Also By Edward Lemond

Birds of Appetite

Journey in Bardo

September Blow Soft

Equal Affection

Nobody Here By That Name (Stories)

Overheard (Poetry)

Verticals of Frye (Editor)

The Breach House Anthology (Editor)

The Breach House Anthology Volume II (Editor)

The Breach House Anthology Volume III (Editor)

The Baptism of Alden Oakes

The Baptism of Alden Oakes

by

Edward Lemond

Attic Owl Books

Lemond, Edward

The Baptism of Alden Oakes

ISBN: 978-0-9780510-9-9

First paperback edition February, 2013

Reprinted, with corrections, February, 2015

Attic Owl Books
379 Beausejour Street
Dieppe, NB E1A 1Y5
Canada

Email: elemond@bellaliant.net

Printed in the United States of America

By www.lulu.com

For Alex and Anna

Contents

Tin Soldier

*T*he driveway was a wind tunnel where drifts could reach four or five feet in the most violent phase of a storm. Alden shovelled for an hour before he reached the front bumper of the buried car. He paused a moment to catch his breath and felt a pressure, a stabbing in his chest. Heartburn he thought. He felt for tender spots along the breastbone and under the rib cage. Because he was sweating he unzipped his coat, and he was hit with such a jolt of pain that he doubled over. For one half second he blacked out. He used the shovel to brace himself against a fall. In a swirl of snowflakes he tried to understand what was happening. Symptoms multiplied like earwigs in the crotch of a lawn chair.

Stay calm, a voice whispered, but the burning sensation in the chest was spreading upward into the arm. Worse than the pain was the sensation of losing all power.

He managed to climb the steps to the house. He stumbled into the little room crammed with muddy boots and crumpled umbrellas. He called Jason but he did not come. The door was half open and snow and wind blew in. He knew it was cold but he could not feel it.

Where is he when I need him?

He had a vision of the end – a remote hillside, a beautiful fall day, trees in the distance, spruce but also birch and maple, in shades of red, orange, and green. He heard someone speak and when he opened his eyes his son, who couldn't have been more than eight years of age, was standing on the copper-trimmed step leading into the main hallway, and behind him the carpet was green, and the bowl on the antique pine table was filled with red apples. "Daddy," he was saying, "Daddy."

Alden was so grateful to hear his voice he was no longer afraid to die.

"I'm having a heart attack. It's important that an ambulance come right away. Do you understand?"

"Yes."

"Dial zero and ask the operator for an ambulance."

He waited for further instructions.

"Please do what I say."

Like a tin soldier he turned on his heel and marched down the hallway into the kitchen. Alden could hear him on the telephone speaking the words he had been given to speak.

Whatever happens now, happens. It's all right.

The next thing he knew he was on a bed of some sort that was being lowered step by step to the sidewalk below and the waiting ambulance. "Take these aspirin," someone said.

Across the street neighbours watched from driveways, lawns, front steps, and open windows. He wanted to protest against being ogled like a fish in a bowl but he had no strength to do so. He felt cold and clammy. His head was resting on a softness that must have been a pillow or a belly, and though he did not know what it was or whose it was he was grateful for that support.

Below him on the steps guiding the descent was a young man with an impressive head of curly black hair. *With hair like that, he doesn't have to worry about penis size.*

The hospital was less than a mile from the house. He lay on some sort of cot with his legs raised a few inches while the man with the soft belly fed him oxygen from a mask. Jason sat up front with the driver, not three feet away. Alden tried to wave but found he could not move his arm. He felt the prick of a needle in his belly.

Have they tied me to the cot? The man with the oxygen told him to lie still. He closed his eyes and sank down into unconsciousness.

It was like being in a boat that was carried along into rapids so rough there was no longer even a prayer of retaining control. Then he felt himself being lifted onto a stretcher and carried through automatic doors into a brightly lit corridor. He sensed light and noise and commotion all around him. Someone was taking his pulse, his blood pressure, hooking him up for an ECG, starting an intravenous. He was a body with a pathology, a machine that needed fixing, and he did not mind such a view of himself. He felt some comfort in the thought that he had no influence whatsoever on the course of events.

"Name," a voice barked.

"Aah," he muttered, unable to move his tongue. "Aah Aah."

"How do you feel," the same voice asked.

He was too confused and groggy to answer. The painkillers were taking effect. A white-coated figure approached the bed. "Well, there's no question you had a heart attack," he said. He looked at a chart on a clipboard and began a lengthy monologue, which made no sense whatsoever. At the end of it he looked at his patient and spoke words that clarified everything magically. "Anterior wall infarction.

About as serious as you can get."

Administrative forces descended on him like a hoard of army ants in full battle fatigues ready to carry him off to their place of worship and devour him. They wanted to know about his family, his job, and his way of life.

"My why ook eave asses," he replied, choosing his words with care.

They looked at one another and smiled. "Dyspnea," someone whispered.

"Children?"

He didn't try to answer.

A nurse in a blue cardigan pointed behind her whereupon everyone looked towards the door and beyond the door into the hallway where Jason was sitting by himself, his chin tucked into his chest, his big head of hair falling over his eyes.

"Siblings? Parents?"

They conferred a very long time while Alden lay as if frozen, without feeling, on a marble bed, convinced from the way in which he was being ignored that he had said or done something so harebrained that they had given up all hope of communicating with him. Then they too were gone, and the nurse gave him a pill to hide under his tongue. When he was asleep she called in the troops, who wheeled him down the hallway to the bank of elevators.

Official Story

*I*t was dark, and he was having trouble waking up. By the side of the bed stood a doctor or doctor's assistant, a big fat man dressed in a long white lab coat. "And how are we tonight," the man said. The voice sounded familiar but no more familiar than a dozen other voices Alden had heard in the last few hours. It was the strange gesture he made with his left hand – three fingers held straight up, the thumb out to the side, the little finger curled in – that finally brought back the image of the white-coated man who had greeted him in emergency the night before with the blunt assessment.

He felt frightened for the first time. "How serious is it?"

The fat man made the same three fingered gesture but with the thumb turned and pointing towards the door of the room. "What do *they* say?"

Alden felt he was sympathetic so he confided in him. "They say I'm losing my memory."

He waved his hand back and forth in front of his face as if swatting a fly. "No need to worry."

"You said it was serious."

"Perhaps I was wrong. They say one thing. I say another. Who are you supposed to believe?"

It was as if the onus were on Alden to decide. But he was sick, and he could not decide. He closed his eyes.

The fat man disappeared, never to be seen again. He had upset Alden terribly at the time but afterwards he felt as if truth itself in a number of long heavy white cloaks piled one on top of the other had met him at the door of the building and handed out facts without false sympathy. He kept hoping he'd come back and tell him what he really thought. He did not care how bleak his message was. *The bleaker the message, the easier it will be to believe.*

The official story, unlike the fat man's, was meant to calm him. He did not believe a word of it. Only the fat man's blunt words remained in his mind as irrefutable. The harder he listened to what was being said the less he grasped. Everyone was smiling and circling around him, pegging him for evacuation, telling him lies. Why not, worse things have been known to happen. Far into the night he tortured himself picturing a massively damaged brain and a shameless conspiracy of doctors, family and friends.

*H*e expected Lise to appear at the door at any moment and set things right, but he needn't have worried. Her flight had been cancelled because of the storm and she had to spend the night in Toronto oblivious to the drama unfolding on the home front. It was late the next morning when she entered the room by which time Alden's speech had become garbled beyond anything that could be accounted for in the usual way – fatigue, drink, apoplexy. She was shocked at the sight of him and did not try to hide the fact.

"I'm losing my memory," he told her. "Otherwise I'm fine."

"Yes, I can see," she said. "You're fine. Wonderful. And tomorrow, if this goes on, you won't know who I am."

"How sad."

She knew exactly what the problem was. He was being shot full of drugs – meperidine to reduce pain, quinidine to control premature ventricular contractions, meprobamate to induce calm during the day and sleep at night. The names and doses were all spelled out on his chart, which she demanded to see. One of these drugs, or some combination, was fucking up his mental process.

What he loved about his wife, among other things, was her stubborn streak, the ruthless, sometimes brutal way she went about finding the truth. Meprobamate was the scientific name for the common tranquilizer valium, and a close reading of the fine print revealed that valium can impair memory function. After explaining what she believed was going on she asked the doctor in charge what he planned to do about it. Much to her annoyance he brushed her concern aside, insisting that valium is not only safe but essential in cases like Alden's.

"You're being alarmist."

"And you're full of shit. Valium may have its value but not in this case. It's doing more harm than good."

Turning to look at an intern standing just behind him the doctor screwed up his courage. "You don't know what you're talking about."

"My husband is a thinker more than a doer. If he can't think he gets depressed. If he has no memory he can't think. You figure it out."

When he saw that she was not just serious but dead serious and not to be swayed by jargon the doctor faltered, caved, and capitulated. From then on things happened more or less as she had predicted they would. Once off the drug Alden's mind cleared and he was himself again. It happened so quickly it seemed a miracle.

He spent three weeks in hospital. His heart attack was now being described as having been serious but not life threatening. The muscle was tender. Scarring was an outcome not to be feared, but welcomed. With that understanding he was free to leave hospital. His instructions upon discharge amounted to the following. As to food, stay on a low-sodium diet – no alcohol, no caffeine. As to exercise, start slowly, walk one block a day, then two, then three. Do not go uphill or into the wind. As to work, not until May or June; then only part-time. Next examination: in one week.

Did he have any questions?

"If the wind is at my back on the way out won't it be in my face on the way back?"

The doctor pushed his glasses down to the tip of his red nose and looked annoyed.

"Don't go walking if it's too windy."

"What about sex?"

"Exercise caution."

"Will it still be sex?"

"You figure it out."

Thunder

*H*e stared at the arm that she held up. It seemed thinner and bonier than before. They clinked glasses. *She's lost weight, why didn't I see it happening?* He had been thinking only of himself because of the heart attack, and now he wanted to make amends.

"Tell me about your trip." She sipped the wine, a mulled wine, hot and spicy the way she liked it at this time of year.

"I spent most of my time at the museum. I didn't see much of the city."

"What was the museum like?"

"It wasn't anything like I had imagined. It was run-down, the walls were crumbling, and mice ran the corridors. The biggest surprise was to find that the library where they keep the manuscripts is a single, small room. Every day I sat with two or three others at the table taking notes because we knew it was a once in a lifetime chance. Cleaning women washed the floor around me. Children played outside in the hallway. Whatever security there might have been was invisible."

"Didn't they worry about the manuscripts?"

"No, they were mounted in plexiglass."

"What did they look like?"

"Not really old like we think of old, just very fragile. The writing was in black ink on golden brown leaves. I found them very beautiful after having seen only black and white photographs."

"Did you see everything you wanted to?"

"I could've spent a year there and barely scratched the surface."

"Will you go back?"

"I'd like to go back in the spring, as soon as we get you back on your feet."

"So soon?"

"The trouble is there are so many others already there ahead of me, better qualified."

"I doubt if that's true."

"We'll see. In the meantime I'll write a paper based on what I've already seen. I've got a pile of notes big enough to drown in."

"What sort of paper?"

"In these early manuscripts there's a lot of feminine imagery for God, all of which disappeared by about the year 200 when the so-called orthodox writings were settled on."

"God the Mother."

"Don't be so snotty."

"I'm not being snotty."

"Let me tell you about a remarkable poem I found, called *Thunder, Perfect Mind*. The voice is the voice of a feminine divine power. Listen to what she says:

I am the first and the last,
I am the honoured one and the scorned one,
I am the whore and the holy one,
I am the wife and the virgin,
I am the barren one and many are my sons,

I am the silence that is incomprehensible,
I am the utterance of my name.

"The unity of opposites. Not very different from Paul when you think about it."

"A lot of what you see in Paul comes from the Jewish Wisdom literature. I'm thinking about Proverbs, Chapter Eight. Sophia and the beginning of time."

"Sophia wasn't a God, unlike your honoured one above."

"I suggest you read the book."

"I will. First thing in the morning." He did not feel like fighting. If she was in the mood, he wasn't. It was Christmas. There was music playing on the radio, somewhere in another room, very faint. *Oh Tannenbaum.*

Alden lugged a new bicycle up from the basement. Lise placed a box containing a toy called Electric Trucking under the tree, with the top removed. Alden tucked a regulation size basketball under the wheel of the bicycle. Lise taped a stocking to the mantel above the fireplace. Alden stuffed the stocking with squares of chocolate, peppermint candies, a pair of dice, and a plastic gorilla.

The room now seemed full and alive with the right kind of spirit. In truth, they had done what they had done and they had left undone what they had left undone.

Breaking the Habit

Early each morning Lise walked Jason to school then continued to her office, another five blocks. Alden was alone in the house. He liked being alone in the house. He did the cooking and the cleaning, the shopping and the errands. If he minded, he did not let on. He had decided to enjoy his little vacation, whether it was deserved or not.

His rehabilitation program was simple. In good weather he took short walks, always sticking close to the house. In bad weather he went to the gym. Lise did not like him to walk to the gym alone. What if he had a heart attack on the way, with no one around until it was too late. On average it takes six minutes for help to reach a heart attack victim in a city the size of theirs, she had read somewhere in a magazine. The brain begins to die in four. You figure it out, she said, glaring at him.

Walnut Street is a quiet street lined with comfortable two-story homes, level most of the way, but hilly at one end, where it rises to a ramshackle building two stories high, the top green, the bottom white. Once a Legion Hall, it was now something called the Sexual Health Centre.

He was always short of breath, his head spinning the way words spin when you press them close together. Sometimes when he went early in the morning Lise would come along to keep him company. Instead of finding comfort in her presence he felt a sort of humiliation in those moments when he had to stop for lack of breath or turn back unable to complete the modest circuit he had set himself.

His self-esteem sunk low as he rehearsed what he could no longer do, what he might never again be able to do. It looked like a very long road ahead, and he didn't know if he had the energy or the courage to sustain the effort. To top it off he found himself smoking again on the sly, stealing butts from ashtrays and smoking in the bathroom when Annalisa wasn't looking. Of course he felt guilty when he did it but he did it anyway. It was stupid, wrong, weak, pathetic, suicidal.

There came a time when he was willing to try anything including enrolling in a stop-smoking workshop. He tried to be good. The doctor asked him to repeat several key phrases – phrases of such simian simplicity that he gagged. Smoking is harmful to my body. I need my body to live. Therefore ... you fill in the blanks.

Whenever he wanted a smoke he was to take three cigarettes, spread them on the table in front of him, and methodically break and crush them. This was called "breaking the habit." Words, like feelings, have power.

Still, he could not stop dreaming up alternatives. In one scenario he's sitting in an expensive restaurant, alone at a table, just opposite a man playing a piano. He's breaking one cigarette after another, ripping them apart and flinging the remains into the air so that bits and pieces of tobacco and paper float into the open piano.

No, no, concentrate. Listen to the doctor's voice. But it was not the doctor's voice he was hearing but a tape of the doctor's voice repeating the idiotic instructions over and over. He sat there with six other suckers, ears cupped, growing angry because he was a human being. He did not have to take advice from a machine whatever the cost, one dollar and twenty-five cents an hour or six fifty or eleven seventy-five. He was not even civil to the receptionist when he walked out, though she was blameless, as far as he knew.

Once outside, he did the first thing that came into his mind. He went into a drugstore, bought a pack, ripped it open and lit up, breathing so deeply he felt a muscle tear in his chest. If he could have got his hands on the smooth-talking community psychologist, the self-styled doctor, he would have strangled him, allowing one twist of the ligature for each fake degree after his name. *If he has to die, so be it. If I have to die, so be it.*

*S*ome friends, recently back from a trip to New York, invited them for dinner. Lesley taught religion at university, in the same department as Lise. Elizabeth was an architect. Judiciously combining their interests, they had done a tour of New York's historic churches. After dinner they showed slides. Alden was bored and kept going to the bathroom. Suspicious, Lise waited outside the door. When he opened the door and stepped into the hall she looked inside and saw the smoke above the mirror, the undeniable proof that made her heart beat fast. Traitor, sneak, liar, imbecile, smoking yourself to death, abandoning me for a moment's escapist pleasure. Widowing me. She went on and on. If you loved me you would not go about killing yourself without even asking.

"I'm killing myself because I can't stand you spying on me."

"Asshole."

"I'm leaving."

"Good riddance."

"Tell your friends I'm very sorry."

"They're not my friends."

"If they're not your friends what the fuck are we doing here."

At this they both burst out laughing because it was true – they were not their friends. They hardly knew them. They were just trying to impress them with their fucking slides. Alden admitted he was in the wrong. He said he'd do better. He'd embrace a new diet as well as a new exercise program. The first requirement, if he wanted to remain in the program, was that he had to stop smoking.

Dropped Plates

Something was bothering Lise but she didn't want to talk about it. But she dropped enough hints that it was soon clear enough. She regretted having to leave Cairo weeks earlier than planned, thanks to Alden's having fallen ill. The research project that had brought her there in the first place (to study the Nag Hammadi texts) was far from complete. But he for his part did not feel guilty. According to him, she should show him some sympathy, etc. According to her, he was floating with the situation and not taking control. They did not see eye to eye. There was electricity in the air.

They argued over little things. What to do about Jason was the bone that was most contentious. They could not agree on a proper course of discipline. How firm to be, where to draw the line, when to say no, when to look the other way. The very concept of discipline, with its connotation of strictness, was something Alden had a hard time getting his head around.

It came to a boil one evening in mid-January when Jason asked a friend for supper and a sleep-over. Jessica was Jason's age, eight going on nine, but bigger – pre-pubescent. Alden had been working upstairs at his desk all day. It was already after six when he came down to get supper – late. Jason and Jessica were busy in the kitchen rooting around in a cookie jar.

Jason had that look of defiance in his eye that he seemed to be cultivating. "We're starving," he said.

"It won't be long," Alden said. "We're having spaghetti and meat sauce."

He put on a pot of water to boil. Lise arrived home just at this moment, entering by the front door. She dumped her bag on the stairway, came down the hall, and listened from the doorway as the scene unfolded.

"We're starving," Jason repeated, for his mother's benefit.

"Yes, we're starving," Jessica chimed in, giggling and looking at Jason, not quite sure what this was all about.

The dishes from breakfast were still in the sink but there was no time to do them now, with everyone clamouring to be fed. He got the onions and garlic and green pepper going, and opened the can of diced tomatoes. He took down enough paper plates for everyone.

"I don't want a paper plate," Jason said, when he saw what his father was attempting to pull. "I want a metal plate."

"The metal plates are in the sink."

Early in their marriage Alden and Lise had acquired a set of cheap porcelain-on-steel plates that came in two sizes, large and small, and six colours, red, blue, green, yellow, orange, and purple. Jason called them metal plates. His favourite colour was red. He always ate from the same small red metal plate.

Jessica put the back of her hand to her mouth and looked at Alden with her dark eyes that reminded him of a hedgehog. "I want a red plate too," she said.

Alden looked at them, and for a second he did not know what he was going to do. Maybe he would scream. Maybe he would open the screen door, go down the steps into the garden and disappear for a few hours, or a few days. Let Lise handle it. The one thing he didn't think he'd do is the thing he did. He went to the sink and washed the little red plate and the big red plate. He rinsed them, dried them, and brought them to the table. He set them down, the little one in front of Jason, the big one in front of Jessica.

"No fair," Jason said. "You gave her the big plate."

As if possessed Jason went to the cupboard, opened the door, and took out several pieces of china. "I'm so angry I'm going to drop these plates on the floor. I don't care if they break."

"You'd better not do that."

"She's a lousy guest. I want her to go home."

Jessica stopped giggling and looked around. Her eyes darted this way and that like fish in a fish tank that have yet to receive any sort of training or even affection.

Lise, in the doorway, had been listening quietly as the little drama played itself out. Suddenly all eyes were on her. Perhaps she knew the way out of the cul-de-sac they found themselves in. She raised an arm as if to brush away a fly that was getting in her hair, flapping her hand open and closed. "Imbecile," she said.

It took Alden a second or two to realize she was talking to him not Jason.

"You let him shit all over you and then you wonder why he behaves the way he does."

"Wait a minute."

"No, I'm talking." She took one step into the room.

"It's always the same story. The boy gets away with murder. I've had it. Jason, put the plates down and go to your room."

Defiant, miserable, torn between his wish to assert himself and his fear of his mother's wrath, Jason hesitated. "You can't make me."

"What did you say?"

"You can't make me."

"If you don't go to your room this very instant you'll live to regret it. I'm not fooling around."

Jason surprised them all, including himself, by looking straight at his mother and saying, "I don't have to."

Lise took two more steps into the room, her hand now balled up in a fist, raised at ear level.

"All right. I'm going." Jason put the plates back on the shelf and closed the cupboard doors.

"Fast, before I get really angry."

"I said I would." He kicked his toe against the chair as he ran by and his howls of pain trailed him up the stairs.

Jane

*T*he weeks went by. Alden graduated from walking to jogging. Every morning, with Sundays off for good behaviour, he was at the track, where he joined half a dozen other men around an abandoned football field. Sundays he'd sometimes go jogging in the park, though at a more leisurely pace. He enjoyed the scent of pine and spruce in the park, and the sound of the white birches. Everybody, everything passed him by – men, women, children, dogs, squirrels, stray leaves fallen from the trees and blown by the wind.

The female body had never looked so good. When he saw melons instead of breasts, he knew he was on the right track, and there was nothing left for him to do but keep ploughing straight ahead.

But one misty Sunday morning towards the end of March the shape that came towards him on the pathway below Prince of Wales Tower was top-heavy to the point of instability, and he muttered to himself, *Screw collegiality, screw the hundred and one unwritten rules of running. There's hardly a soul in sight. This once, just this once I want to get an eye-full. It's not against the law, is it? What can she do, scream? I don't think so.*

In the end he was so busy getting his eye-full that he didn't recognize the woman until she came to a full stop, not a yard away. Dropping her arms to her sides, she took a deep breath, and said in a voice that was all too familiar, "Hello Alden."

In a panic he tried to grasp what was happening. *How does she know my name? Is she trying to pick me up?*

He looked again but higher up and almost fainted, because it was Jane, a colleague of Lise's at the university. More than a colleague. A good friend.

"I didn't know you ran."

"What about you? Since when are you running?"

"Doctor's orders."

"Which way are you going?"

"I don't know, what about you?"

"I'm going home."

"Mind if I tag alone?"

"Not at all. But I have no intention of slowing down for you."

Sabrina, Jane's daughter, was eight months younger than Jason but a head taller. She was standing at the top of the stairs when they came in. "Is that you mama?"

"Yes love." Jane's voice was always fresh, as if it were part of the job description.

"Who's that man with you?"

"It's Alden."

"Oh."

Alden went to the bottom of the stairs and looked up at Sabrina. "Hi."

When she saw him Sabrina lost interest and returned to her room. Jane led the way into the kitchen, which was at the back of the house. She poured two glasses of orange juice and handed one to Alden.

"So, how are you? I guess you had a scare."

"Better, much better. I run, I watch my diet, I try not to get too excited."

"Any news from Lise?"

"She called Friday to say she had arrived safely. She sounded very happy."

"She's a fanatic for work."

"What can I say? It's in her blood."

"Eggs allowed in this new diet of yours?"

"I'm allowed one egg a week. More than one, I'm risking life and limb."

"I'm sure we can manage that." She cracked three eggs and beat them hard with a fork. "You get one third."

"I can live with that."

She sliced a mushroom for the omelette. "Or we could just skip the omelette and go upstairs."

"There's an idea. But isn't, you know, Sabrina upstairs?"

"Sabrina's a big girl. She knows I have men friends."

"I suppose she has her own music, or something. To drown out, you know, the noise."

Jane laughed because he was so shy. "If you don't want to, just say so."

His face got redder and redder. He thought if he stopped talking his heart might stop thumping and scaring the shit out of him. "It's not that I don't want to."

"Look, let's forget it. Some other time. I'm hungry."

"Is it okay with you if I, you know, stay?"

"Hey, a promise is a promise."

Frail Man

*A*t first he seemed interested, even excited, looking out the window at the Sears building, the container terminal at the edge of Bedford Basin, the long, low bridge across the narrows, and the floating dock in the middle of the Basin that seemed to have no good reason to be there. Once past the town of Bedford, though, heading into the interior of the province, with its vast stretches of woods, broken at rare intervals by the blinking lights at a crossroad, he grew bored. Wired to his Sony Walkman, nodding his head to the rhythm of the music, he closed everything else out. It was left up to Alden then to stare out the window at the passing scenery.

The train would take them to Wolfville and back. Alden's plan was to explore the town, have lunch, and after lunch walk out to a beach and watch the tide come in. Or go out. He thought if they did things together they'd bond. With memories in common they'd find it easier to talk.

At Windsor Junction the train stopped to admit a frail, small-boned, dark-skinned man, of indefinite age, who came up the aisle, and, without looking at them, took the window seat opposite where they were sitting. He carried nothing with him except a paperback book, which, once seated, he placed on his lap and covered with his two large, bony hands. On his square head he wore a Greek fisherman's hat, blue with a miniature gold braid on the down-turned brim.

Reaching into the canvas bag on the floor Alden felt for the plastic thermos he had brought. He held the inverted top, now serving as a cup, in his left hand while he poured with his right. With the pitching and rolling of the train, the coffee in the cup did not spill but instead formed perfect little rippling circles on top, like waves that had already traveled great distances.

As if this were the cue he needed, this pouring of the coffee, the conductor rose and came forward to collect a fare from the frail man. Alden sipped his coffee and watched the unfolding drama. Jason, beside him, listened to his music.

The frail man coughed violently. Unable to speak because of the coughing, he looked across at Alden as if to implore his forgiveness. Alden stared back, unaware of anything that needed his forgiveness. The man got and went to the back of the train, where there was a toilet.

On the faded, cushioned seat the book he had left behind was turned so that Alden could see the front cover. In the middle of the cover was a black shape, circular but with ragged edges all around. In the middle of the black shape was a single eye in the form of a band of orange surrounding a spot of green. The title of the book was *Mystics & Zen Masters*. The author's name was Thomas Merton.

When the frail man did not return to his seat, Alden reached across and picked up the book. He was startled to see that every page was marked in a heavy, dark pencil with many words circled. Here and there whole sentences or paragraphs were underlined. He turned the pages, but when he tried reading some of the underlined material it was like reading Latin. His eyes ached. *I've been drinking too much coffee.*

With an effort he deciphered one line. "Zen is not attained by mirror-wiping meditation." *Now what the hell is that supposed to mean.*

He went forward to inspect the front of the train. A window with two panes looked into a compartment where the engineer sat, in a corner to one side, down in a sort of pit. Without knocking, Alden opened the door and went inside.

The engineer did not turn around to see who it was. Alden faced a curved, green-tinted window through which he could see out onto the tracks ahead. Below the window was an assortment of black, grimy, antiquated dials and levers. The seat consisted of a cushion on top of an orange crate.

"How far you going," the engineer asked.

Alden had to shout above the noise. "Wolfville!"

Everything was close and coming at him so fast he felt overwhelmed. Whole stands of trees flashed by, and sudden clearings. It was as if he was about to be engulfed at every moment, by trees, or mountains, or clouds, but he kept breaking through, into new perils. The tracks were like traces of bullets coming at him with great speed and then vanishing below, leaving him, miraculously, untouched.

Hunched down in his corner, in his little world of grease and grime, the engineer seemed vulnerable, even shy, sniffing the air like a mouse wary of attack. Yet when he spoke, he spoke in a normal voice and had no trouble making himself heard.

The door opened, and the conductor came in. He held a newspaper in one hand, tightly rolled up like a stick, or a policeman's baton.

There was barely room for the three of them.

"We on time today, Ross, or late as usual." It sounded like a statement but it was a question. He tapped the engineer on the shoulder with the newspaper.

Ross did not take his eye off the road ahead.

Alden leaned into the window and resumed his watch.

The conductor spoke to him in a low voice, as he leaned into the window with Alden. "Up ahead, another mile, there's an old guy lives in a shack. All alone. When I say shack, I mean shack. Primitive. Every day, and this is where it gets a mite queer, every day, without fail, he's gotta have his newspaper. Why does he need a newspaper, I ask you, livin' where he lives. He don't belong to this world. But like I say, it don't matter to me. To each his own."

"Does he farm, or what?"

"Farm? Couldn't farm that land even if he wanted to. Couldn't do no farmin' there no more than I could go fishin' in my kitchen sink."

"What does he do then?"

"Nothin' much, far as I can tell. I see him out there choppin' wood once in a while."

"How does he survive?"

"Welfare. Damn people down in Halifax that hands out all that welfare money."

"Better than leaving him to rot, I guess."

"Don't do nobody no good. The poor man's just goin'to hell the hard way."

Ross cleared his throat. "One of these days I expect we'll see him stretched out across the tracks up yonder. Wouldn't surprise me at all."

They rounded a bend and started down a long straight narrow section, closed in by the thickening spruce. Opening a window, the conductor let in a rush of air and the loud clack-clack of the wheels on the tracks.

In a clearing a dog, with the head of a collie and the body of a cocker spaniel, barked furiously, as the train bore down on her yet again, as it did every day. The conductor held the rolled-up newspaper out the window and, at the appointed moment, released it.

A man stood in the doorway of the shack, rubbing his eyes, not even looking up. Before the paper hit the ground the pages began to unroll and scatter in all directions.

The conductor shouted something into his cupped hands. The man waved.

The image of the man in the doorway of the shack haunted Alden. The shack was no bigger than an outhouse, with a tin roof and sides covered in tarpaper. The clearing was a dump – rusted-out car frames, piles of old tires, discarded mattresses, television sets, beer bottles spilling out of shrivelled cardboard boxes, unopened loaves of bread, streamers of toilet paper, whiskey bottles.

He should make an effort, pick himself up, start over. Do

something. But he's beyond that. He's finished. Worst of all, he knows it.

Perhaps he's at peace with himself.

But if so, I do not see it written on his face.

Piping Plover

*C*anada Day weekend Alden and Jason camped in a provincial park outside Chester, Nova Scotia. From the camp they took day trips, exploring the coastline. They followed a back road to Peninsula Farm, outside Lunenburg, and bought a bucket of blueberry ice cream. They visited a park called *The Ovens* south of Lunenburg and peered into caves carved in the face of the cliff by the force of the sea. They stopped for lunch at Linden Lodge in Petite Riviere, in a lovely home on a hill above the bay.

Every day – weather permitting – they went swimming in the frigid Atlantic.

The water at Risser's Beach was no colder than half a dozen other places they had tried, but the fog made it seem so. They followed the boardwalk towards the mud flats where a few dozen people were digging for clams. A sign warned them not to disturb the nesting sights of the piping plover, an endangered species. The nests were hidden in the thin grasses of the dunes just below the boardwalk.

Alden saw something grey flit down and away, into the grasses. He heard its low, sharp whistle. He was curious and excited. *Where do they make their nests? With what? Are there eggs in the nests? How many? When is hatching time?*

The area was remote. The clam diggers were some distance away, absorbed in their task. As carefully as he could, he stepped through the grasses towards where he heard the sound coming from.

"It's not allowed." Alden wondered where the words were

coming from. Some inner voice, he thought.

Jason would not budge from the boardwalk, though Alden motioned for him to follow. He thrust his hands into the pockets of his windbreaker.

"It's all right. Just be careful."

"It's not allowed." The look on his face was as troubled as the dark sky over the hills beyond his shoulder.

Alden felt sorry for him because he seemed to be in so much danger himself – as much danger as the bird. But where was the danger coming from? Alden stopped a moment and looked around. He tried to imagine what he looked like, from his son's point of view. What he sounded like.

He's developing a mind of his own, is the remarkable thing. Alden did not believe he could take any credit. Was he wrong to think so? Wasn't it his job to help shape the process? Should he apologize for doing what came naturally?

Please Have Mercy!

*A*lthough not a hard worker, Jason did well in school. Everything came easily to him. On occasion, though, his strong sense of right and wrong got him into trouble. If he thought a teacher unfair in her judgments, or inconsistent in his discipline, he was quick to take it upon himself to raise an objection. The teacher in question rarely appreciated the intervention.

Lise thought he was foolish to stick his neck out, when there was nothing to be gained. He was being defiant for the sake of being defiant, she thought. Power lay with the teacher, a fact he would have to learn to live with. Alden approved Jason's sense of right and wrong, but not the way he made his case.

"All you'll end up getting for your troubles is a bad name."

"You always side with her."

It was true. At this time he had a sense of himself as playing a very passive role. Still recovering from his heart attack, out of work, he had never felt more hemmed in. Being at home all day left him feeling – sluggish. *How nice it would be to walk calmly away, and never look back. Drop in at a movie, breeze through a shopping mall, buy a new pair of shoes.*

All he wanted was a little vacation from things – from cries and dishes, from shoelaces. He'd rather not look at them. He was fed up – with his face, his fingernails, his shadow. But something held him in its grip. Something shoved him into supermarkets, into shoe stores, into fast food chains with their soggy French fries.

In July they rented a cottage at the ocean, near Lunenburg. It was to be a sort of retreat and re-grouping. Jason could put school and everything to do with school out of his mind, and Alden promised Lise he would not work on his play if she would not speak to him or ask his opinion about anything having to do with Gnosticism. The point was to relax and enjoy Nature with a capital N.

Lise, the one who least expected to, enjoyed herself immensely. Intense, moody, with a temper larger than life, she was also a ham. She'd listen to people on the beach and imitate their speech and manners in her deadpan way. Alden was amused, perplexed, and charmed. There was something solid, something indestructible, he imagined, at the centre of her being, which he held in direct contrast to his own feeling that in him, at the core, there was something lacking. He was not fully alive. Convictions of being drained of energy alternated with feelings of depression. He had lost his instinct in this matter, and he could not reason his way to any clear picture. She infuriated him because she seemed so extremely composed. He tried to remember what had fascinated him the first time they met. She had the most beautiful eyes he'd ever seen. They looked much darker than he had ever known them to be.

The last night at the cottage there was a cold wind across the water. Jason needed an extra blanket when he went to bed. Lise tended the fire, while Alden opened a second bottle of wine. Without having given it much thought, he began talking about the idea of having a second child. Lise rolled her eyes.

"I'm serious."

"I'm sure you are."

"There just seems to be – something missing."

"If it's important to you, by all means, go ahead and pursue it."

"Pursue it?"

"A pregnancy is out of the question. You know that."

"Pray tell why, Nancy."

"If you want to have another child, be my guest. But don't expect me to take another year off to look after it."

"I didn't know you felt that way."

"Welcome to the real world."

She stirred the fire. He closed his eyes and basked in the glow.

The Only Thing She Needs

*T*he person Alden talked to at the Children's Aid Society was a Mrs. Hobson. As long as one of them, it didn't matter which, planned to remain at home, Mrs. Hobson saw no reason not to encourage them to foster a child. Once this was understood, Alden felt a great burden off his shoulders. Something new was coming into his life. He had not realized how depressed he had been, at such a deep level he hadn't even been aware of it.

He made an application, which Lise signed off on with a notable lack of enthusiasm. It wasn't long before they learned of a child who seemed to be just what they were looking for. She was six years old, from a farm outside Digby. Her mother had died of cancer and her father had a drinking problem. She had lived awhile with neighbours, but this had not worked out. At the moment she was living in Halifax, staying in a group home, awaiting a suitable placement. Finding much in this narrative to interest them, Alden and Lise made an appointment to learn more.

Her name was Gabriele, with one 'l'. Gabriele La Blanc. Not Le, La. Though she was the right age, she might prove difficult, Mrs. Hobson warned. She'd already run away a number of times. "Once they develop that pattern, it's hard to break. Also, she's very shy. You'll find that she won't talk much at all."

But the more he thought about it and talked it over with Lise, the more convinced Alden was that Gabriele was right for them, and they were right for her. She was a bright girl, Mrs. Hobson had said, and only needed a lot of patience and understanding.

It was a warm, wet Saturday, in the month of August, when Lise and Alden and Jason went to bring Gabriele home to stay with them. Mrs. Hobson had a few pieces of last-minute advice. Don't make a fuss. She won't respond to that sort of thing at all. Make her feel she's part of the family, but at the same time don't force her into a role she's not ready for. Don't ask too many questions. Don't put too much pressure on her. Her passivity may fool you: don't let it. She may be quiet but she's quick. Mentally, she's all there. Emotionally, she's got some catching up to do. The last few months have not been easy. She has to know she can trust you. This type will often blossom in a most unexpected and delightful way. Etc.

Gabriele did not say anything on the drive home. She sat in the back of the car with Jason and looked out the window. When Lise turned around and said something, she pretended she hadn't heard. She pressed her nose flat against the glass.

After lunch Alden took the two children shopping, to a new supermarket he wanted to have a look at. Inside the store, he found himself buying and buying, with no idea what she might want or like. She would not answer when he spoke to her. She would not look at him. She walked ahead, through rows and rows of potato chips, cookies, candies, and soft drinks.

He hurried to keep up with her. One last time he bent down and asked her if there was anything she wanted. She looked at him and spoke in the clearest, most grown-up little voice. "I want some instant potatoes." *Now where the hell did that come from?*

What shocked him was not that she had spoken, for she was bound to speak sooner or later, but that she had expressed such a well thought out, clear desire. He would have expected chips or coke. It was as if a child of three, who had never spoken a word in her life, had suddenly announced at breakfast table, I'd like another egg. It had that same kind of startling effect. He breathed a sigh of relief.

She'll be fine, if we give her time.

The Worst Thing About Sleeping

Sunday morning Lise and Jason went bicycling, while Alden remained at home with Gabriele. Gabriele watched television. Colour was new to her. Sesame Street, which she had thought she had outgrown, was fun again. Mr. Rogers had more colour in his voice, though she'd always known it was there because of the words he spoke. But when Sergeant Preston came on and it was not in colour, she was upset. She looked around for the first time all morning to see if someone could come and fix it.

Sergeant Preston was her favourite show. In the cold, close, scenic quarters of the Far North, just when everything seemed lost, he made it all turn out right in the end. She wanted it to be in colour too.

The first week she would not read a book, nor would she go riding with Jason on the new bicycle they had bought, nor would she go swimming with them at the beach. She watched television, she nibbled her food, and she slept.

She slept fitfully. When she woke and saw that it was still dark, she cried to herself. She listened to the sound of the window rattling in the wind. She wished she could fall asleep again and wake up in her mother's house, surrounded by woods, and her mother not dead. She did not like the house where she was now.

Tomorrow was the first day of school.

Stephen, the boy who lived in the farmhouse across the road from the house where she was born, was her best friend. They rode their bicycles down the hill to the main highway, kicking up as much dust as they could. Stephen's bike had high handlebars and a red flag behind, in case he stayed out till after dark.

She wanted to go to the same school he went to. Or for him to go to the same school she went to. She would not be so afraid even though it was a new school and even though the boys and girls were all strange, city-bred, city-reared. But Stephen would know what to say to city kids. He always knew what to say. He could be funny if he wanted to be, but he was not mean, no.

If she said she had a headache, maybe they would let her stay home. But if she caused too much trouble, they might say they could not keep her. Then she would have to go back to that place on Barrington Street. A group home, it was called. It was more like a jail. She'd run away, more than once.

She'd run away when she was staying with Howard and Edna, Stephen's parents, after her father couldn't keep her because he drank too much. It wasn't that Edna was ever cross or mean or anything. If she said she couldn't have something, or couldn't do something, she always tried to explain why not. It didn't matter that she was a little older than most mothers, or a little heavier, or a little slower. And she still liked Stephen even though they got into more fights than they used to. And sure Howard was gruff sometimes, but he wasn't mean. She knew the difference between gruff and mean.

The worst thing about sleeping was that you had no idea what time it was. You could guess sometimes if you looked at the window but with the streetlight shining through the curtain she could not expect to see the dawn until it was really late. She had the terrifying thought that it might already be time to get out of bed. She knew they were going to get up early, to make sure there was plenty of time to get ready for school.

She turned over in bed and tried to make the time pass more slowly. The only help to her imagination was the memory of the Bible stories her mother had told her. She remembered the story of Noah's Ark and the story of Rebekah at the well and the story of Job and the story of the three wise men from the East who came looking for the baby Jesus. But most of all she remembered the story of Jonah – how he fled his call to preach, how he was swallowed by a fish for three days and three nights, how he came to the city Ninevah and preached and had success in spite of himself, and how he was angry when God did not keep his promise to destroy the city.

The boy in the other room coughed again. It was not Stephen. She was afraid he would wake up and it would be time for her to wake up too. Then he stopped coughing and it was quiet again.

She waited for the sounds of morning – the squeak of the bed, the creak of the floorboard, the lights in the crack under the door, the toilet flushing. But they did not come. Only the boy's hacking cough, followed by more silence. She drifted into sleep again, and she dreamed that she was sleeping in the shade of a magical plant, which was as tall as a tree but shaped like a mushroom, and when she opened her eyes, her mother was smiling down at her.

Spinning Wheel

*A*lden pulled into the parking lot across the road from the fairgrounds. A young man with an orange-tipped baton directed him where to park. Jason had his door open before the car came to a full stop. Gabriele sulked in her corner of the back seat. Alden tapped on the half-open window. "Is everything okay?"

With her chin in her chest she looked like a puppet held together by string, after the string has been cut. "I don't want to go to no fair."

"Oh, come on."

"I'm bored."

"How can you be bored until you come along and give it a try?"

"It's stupid."

More sad than angry Alden called Jason, who had made his way to the edge of the road and was looking across at the lights of the midway. "We're going home."

"I don't want to go home."

"Do what I say."

Jason sat in the front seat because he didn't want to be near Gabriele. Alden started the car and began to back out.

"Okay, I'll come." Her quick little voice had a question mark at the end of it.

Alden held tight to the steering wheel until he was calm again. What she was saying, he tried to convince himself, was that she was willing to give him the benefit of the doubt. *She's fickle, well so what, if it means she's coming around.*

51

At first it did not look like it. Plodding through the mud to get to the fairgrounds was pretty grim. The noise of the tractors, warming up for a race, made her grimace and cover her ears. On the carrousel there was not the hint of a smile. But on the Ferris wheel, as she swung high and dropped to earth, she saw him, and something in his look, in the way he was standing, his hand touching his forehead as if in salute, must have given her comfort, for when he waved, she waved back.

On the tilt-a-whirl, squeezed between Jason and another boy, braids flying, she had the beginning of a grin on her face. Coming down from the ride, brushing loose strands of hair from her forehead, she was a different Gabriele, a happier, brighter Gabriele.

But then this new Gabriele, again, did not last long – she was so perishable. It was too stupid for words. As she was waiting in a line to get a stick of cotton candy, she turned to watch a group of boys approaching from the direction of the Ferris wheel. By the time she recognized them from school it was too late. One of them said something about her braids, and they all laughed. They were long, thick braids, and the boys thought they'd cut them off, tied them together, and make a super-duper jumping rope.

They were on their own, the devilish boys – excited, animated, willing to try everything, do everything, rushing from ride to ride, adventure to adventure, not quite old enough to cause real trouble, but old enough to want to and to believe they had it in their power to do so.

"Where's Jason," said Jimmy Rafuse, who had the reputation of being the best hockey player in school, though he was only in the fourth grade.

"Feelin' up the girls on the tilt-a-whirl, I bet," said little Davey Cahill, who was a Jehovah's Witness and went to church three times a week, sometimes four.

"Forget about Jason," said Johnny MacKenzie, the youngest of them at seven, but big enough, strong enough and cocky enough, with his genuine Swiss army knife, to contend with Jimmy for leadership of the gang. "We don't need any sissies."

"Jason's no sissie," said Gabriele, and the boys laughed louder and ran off.

Unaware that he was being talked about, Jason was having the time of his life in the 'Hall of Mirrors,' but now Alden called him to come out, and he couldn't pretend forever that he didn't hear. So they left the midway and went to the big red-painted barns in the back of the fairgrounds, where animals were kept for the viewing pleasure of the public.

There were goats in the first barn, kept in a fenced-in area in the middle of the straw-covered, cement floor. When people approached, they raised themselves up, with their front legs on top of the fence, to be petted and fed. They were clean and short-haired and did not like to eat plain straw, only the flowering top.

The next barn housed cattle. One big pink puffed-up face after another stared blankly at them. Gabriele hurried through without stopping, followed by Alden. Jason lingered, wanting to discover for himself, in the quiet of a private moment, if what the animal in the stall in the corner had grown were wrinkled utters or the biggest, the most gigantic, pair of testicles he had ever laid eyes on in his life.

Outside the third and last barn Alden bumped into Harold Rafuse, the father of one of the boys who had had such fun teasing Gabriele earlier. Leaving his father, Jason went on inside the barn, where he found Gabriele attempting to feed one of the horses, a grey mare. The holes in the wire-mesh were so small, however, that Gabriele was having trouble pushing the twigs of straw through to the horse. In frustration the animal, her lip pulled up, dragged her exposed teeth roughly up and down the wire, until it seemed she might hurt herself.

"Back off," Jason said, and Gabriele wasn't sure if he meant her or the horse. The horse was restless, and probably angry, moving back and forth from the wire-mesh in front to the little window in the back of her cell, through which she could see, with her big, brown, bulging eye, across to the next barn, where the cattle made low sounds like cries of distress or inchoate warnings.

Helpful Jason came forward with another handful of straw, pushed it in a little, and stood aside to let Gabriele to finish the job. The horse took it roughly, and Gabriele jumped back. She was so huge, so wild, Gabriele was a little afraid. The straw had the sound of fresh breakfast cereal in her mouth.

Alden stood just inside the barn, watching. Jason said, "Dad's here. Let's go." But Gabriele kept her eye fastened to the grey mare as Jason tugged at her elbow, trying to pull her away. The horse pushed her body lengthwise against the wire, tight as a cat, and watched as her new friend was being taken from her.

For the first time she was quiet.

On the way to the car, near the road by the main entrance, they came to another barn, this one with a sign above the door that said, 'Home Crafts (Women's Work).' Inside, on a scrubbed cement floor, which felt cold at first, different kinds of wheels had been set in motion. There were displays of wool spinning, of weaving, of silk screening. There was a woman selling dolls made from husks of corn. There was a woman standing behind a table of eggs, which she had hollowed out and decorated, using decals and dime store jewellery. When Alden asked if they were hand painted she said, "Good Lord, no, then they'd cost at least a hundred dollars." There was a woman shaping clay on a machine that she powered by foot and another kneading dough for bread.

Someone pressed a ball of wool into Gabriele's hand and she accepted it, but only because she felt trapped. "I like your dress, honey," the woman said, and Gabriele blushed and looked away.

"Can we go now," she said.

All the way home she held the ball of wool clutched in her fist, as if it were her most prized possession.

What Does the Witch Need?

Gabriele's birthday was in two days. Lise went shopping for a new supply of birthday napkins and birthday hats. Alden decorated the dining room, with balloons and multi-coloured crepe paper. Friends were invited, the few Gabriele had met and didn't seem to be afraid of: Sabrina, Jason's friend, who was eight; Jane, Sabrina's mother; Lesley and Elizabeth, friends of the family, fond of children, though they had none of their own.

At bedtime she lay awake, unable to sleep. In the dark she looked at Lise with a boldness that only darkness allowed. "Is there something you want to say," Lise asked.

"I was thinking …"

"Yes."

"There's this ad on T.V.?"

"Yes."

"When the child has a birthday they make the cake and everything?"

"Uh-huh."

"Could we, do that?"

"Where would all this, uh, take place?"

"MacDonald's."

Lise felt like one of those celebratory balloons, pricked and deflated. Not one of her negative feelings, however, did she allow herself to express in front of the child. Nor did Alden, in his turn. It's her birthday, she has every right. Nevertheless, they were less than enthusiastic as the day approached.

Previous preparations were scrapped. Lesley stayed home. So did Jane. Alden took down the crepe paper. Lise put away the candles. The six of them, Gabriele, Jason, Lise, Alden, Sabrina, and Elizabeth (good, kind Elizabeth, who came along simply to augment the ranks, without expecting to enjoy herself for one second), piled into the car, drove across town not to the nearest but to the nicest MacDonald's, put on hats, sang songs, finishing with 'Happy Birthday' when the MacDonald's girl in her uniform came through the door with cake, clapped when Gabriele succeeded, after two tries, in blowing out the candles, and in general had a much better time than any of the grown-ups had expected to have. Gabriele's face was aglow. This was not like in a commercial at all. This was real.

The child has a mind of her own, after all. Good for her.

Gabriele: "You ask me, what does the witch need?"

Lise: "Okay, what does the witch need?"

Gabriele: "A black cat."

Lise: "Why does she need a black cat?"

Gabriele: "So she can make black catsoup."

Lise: "Ugh!"

Halloween

*H*alloween was just around the corner. Gabriele said, "Read me a scary story." Lise read her a story called 'Mrs. Gertrude' from the Brothers Grimm.

Once upon a time there was a little girl and she was obstinate and wilful and did not obey her parents when they spoke to her. What good can come to such a child? One day she said to her parents, 'I've heard so much talk about Mrs. Gertrude I want to go and see her. People say her house is very strange and I've become curious.' Her parents strictly forbade her and said, 'Mrs. Gertrude is an evil woman who does wicked things. If you go there, you are no longer our child.' But the girl paid no attention, and though her parents had told her no, went anyway, and when she got to Mrs. Gertrude, Mrs. Gertrude said, 'Why are you so pale?' 'Ah,'the girl answered, trembling all over, 'because I'm frightened at the things I've seen.' 'What have you seen?' 'I saw a black man on your stairs.' 'That was a collier.' 'Then I saw a green man.' ' That was a hunter.' 'And then I saw a man red as blood.' 'That was a butcher.' 'Ah, but, Mrs. Gertrude, it made my skin crawl when I looked through the window and didn't see you but it must have been the devil himself with his head on fire.' 'Oho,'said she, 'so you have seen the witch in her true ornament. I have been expecting you a long time and have hankered for you. You are goi ng to brighten up my house for me.' And she changed the little girl into a log and threw it into the fire. And when it was a full glow she sat down beside it, warmed herself, and said, 'There now, isn't that nice and bright!' And the little girl was no more.

Gabriele wanted to hear the story over and over again. Lise tired the third or fourth time through and gave the book to Gabriele. "Here, you read for a while. I'll listen."

Sitting on the couch in her pajamas, her legs crossed and tucked under her, looking very grown up, she read the words aloud, to anyone who cared to listen. Then she went back and read them again. When she found a word too difficult to pronounce, she was not shy about asking for help; never, however, did she allow the meaning of the word, which was hers and hers alone, to be explained. "Oh, now I remember," was her invariable reply, even when it was the third or fourth time she had asked about the same word. Having broken her reading to ask for help, she would go back and start again from the beginning – never where she had left off. In her voice was more excitement that she had brought to bear on anything since coming to live with them.

*J*ason, in black pants and black turtleneck sweater, a bright yellow handkerchief over his nose and mouth, was a robber. Gabriele, in a black slip that belonged to Lise (hung from the shoulders like a dress), a purple shawl over the shoulders and chest, a black wig, red lipstick, and large glass rings on the fingers of both hands, was a rich lady.

What was the significance of Gabriele's choice? I'm rich, I don't need nothin' from nobody.

Did she have a last minute change of mind? Yes. She hated the wig, it didn't feel right, it kept sliding off. The rings, as if on command, popped apart every so often. Instead of a rich lady, she wanted to go as Batman.

Lise did not have a Batman costume. Gabriele insisted she could not go except as Batman. Lise borrowed a pair of tights from Jane, trimmed the black slip to the size of a cape and turned it around, made a mask out of construction paper, which, however, looked, when finished, more like a helmet a hot suffering medieval knight might wear than anything else. But it was the best she could do, given the time constraint.

Gabriele followed darkly behind Jason, at a safe distance, rushing up at the last moment with her bag held open to be filled. Nobody could guess what she was supposed to be, she was in and out so quickly. But if she minded, she did not let on.

The Words

*I*n school Gabriele continued to be labelled shy. This was true enough as far as it went; but behind the shyness was a much simpler reality: she was scared. The rows of desk, stuffed with notebooks, crayons, sneakers and gym shorts, scared her. The poems on the flip chart in the corner of the room, which she believed, mistakenly, that she was supposed to memorize, scared her. The alphabet on the wall above the blackboard, each letter in a little square, each square framed elaborately by a corresponding plant or animal, scared her. The teacher's gentle probing, randomly administered, scared her. Even the paper flowers pasted on the windows of the room scared her, because they were not real. But one day, when the teacher came to class with a real plant for her desk, she wasn't scared. "Is that a flower," she asked, pointing to the yellow furry many-tiered outcropping in the middle of the plant. "It's called a zebra," the teacher answered, happy for the question – any question from this newcomer.

She was falling rapidly, fatally behind in her work. She had trouble paying attention. She would stare out the window as if nothing were happening, as if no one were there. At home Lise tutored her in some subjects, Alden in others. She had the ability but not the motivation. Her mind was elsewhere, and elsewhere was all blurry.

They made an appointment to talk with the teacher. The child was shy, it was agreed. She had to be encouraged to come out of her shell. "What do you suggest," Lise said. "Pack a little something special in her lunchbox – a bag of chips, a pack of chewing gum, a bag of jelly beans, whatever – which she can share with other children and make friends."

"But would she," Alden said.

"It's a question of opening up lines of communication," the teacher said.

As it turned out there were plenty of lines all right, but more like fault lines, as this kid or that kid came up, snatched a piece of gum or candy, and ran back to where he had come from, to resume playing as before, that much richer. Perhaps a child or two did stay behind, to talk, according to teacher's instructions; but to no avail, because Gabriele would stubbornly refuse to say anything in reply.

The teacher conceived an alternative strategy. "Let's see if we can find a part for her in the Christmas concert," she said. "Working on something like this, together with the other children, she won't feel so left out."

"What I'm afraid of is that this might just make her feel more frightened," Lise said. "More put upon."

"Let's think of an easy part for her," the teacher said. "She could be an animal. A sheep."

Lise moaned. "A sheep? Won't that make her feel foolish?"

"Well, then, she could be one of the three wise men. They don't have much to say."

"All right, I suppose we should give it a try."

The first wise man was so say: *Where is He that is born King of the Jews.* The second was to say: *For we have seen His star in the*

East. And the third was to say: *And are come to worship Him.* Gabriele, it was decided, was to play the third wise man. If she found herself unable to deliver her line, they could go right on without her and, more than likely, no one would notice the difference.

Gabriele did not want to do it at all, at first. But when she began to think about what her words were, which she was being given to say, when she began to be able to focus on the words and put everything else out of her mind, then she dared to tell herself that maybe she could do it. Just maybe. She did not say yes or no, which was as close as she could come to committing herself.

And are come to worship Him. At the first rehearsal she refused to say anything but practiced her words inwardly, not moving her lips or giving any outward sign that she was even aware of what she was being asked to do. She stood where she was supposed to stand but did not move – like a pillar of salt. She had to be dragged off the stage when her part was over.

Later, on the way home from school, playing hopscotch, watching television, taking a bath, reading a book, lying in bed – she found herself repeating the words to herself over and over. Sometimes she no longer knew what they meant, only that they were magical and touched something in her that was deeper than she knew. Saying them, she always thought first of her mother, because her mother would talk like that, with the same light, sweet rhythm as in the Biblical words; and when she thought of her mother she felt at home, safe, secure, free.

The words were something no one else had. For that reason, whoever was there when she thought of them seemed to share a little in their magic. She thought of them when Annalisa thrust her powdered hands into the great mound of bread dough, lifting and turning and pounding it on the counter by the stove in the kitchen: pounding it down with the heels of her hands, folding and pounding it down again very patiently until it grew elastic; always using oil at the end, instead of flour, against the stickiness, for if she used too much flour, she said, the bread would be crumbly in the middle, and difficult to cut. She thought of them when she was saw Alden sitting at his desk, his thoughts slipping away from him and weaving in and out of their own accord, until he was almost unconscious of anything else. She thought of them when Jason called her outside to play touch football; when he showed her how to hold the ball with the fingers spread out evenly on the seam to throw a spiral with an overhand motion; when he said, "That's okay, you're getting really good," if the ball slipped off her fingers; but when some boy from down the block came to play and he sent her away, because she did not "play right," then she thought of them fiercely, as a weapon.

The words gave her something to hold on to, when she was with the ones she *did not* like. When Jane came by, Saturday afternoons, to see Lise, and they'd sit in the kitchen, slicing apples with a knife, talking in hushed tones and cackling in see-saw pendulum. Their thoughts seemed to curl and arch, like a cat getting set to spring. Later, Jason and Sabrina would come rushing in, up the stairs to play together alone; and if Gabriele came up, they'd tell her to go away. Or they'd tell her to come into the bathroom with them and close the door and watch how they could pee sitting backward on the toilet and they'd make her do it too, even though it hurt her more than it did them, because she was smaller. And if it got all over the floor they'd laugh and say she had to clean it up or they'd tell and say she did it.

Or when Lesley and Elizabeth came for coffee and cake, Friday evenings, and Alden would tell her to go upstairs and play because the grown-ups wanted to "chat" awhile. But Jason didn't want to play, because he was listening to a record or doing his stamp collection, and the television was downstairs, so she could not even watch the shows she liked. She would lie on her back with a book but she couldn't really understand what was being said.

Or when the children from down the block came knocking, weekdays after school, or Saturday mornings; or when she ran into them in the playground at recess; or when she met them on the side of the hill where they went tobogganing, coming straight up the middle of the hill, blocking her way – blocking everyone's way.

She thought of them too when she was alone: when she put on the new sneakers with the grey soles so shiny she could hardly bear to take the first step. Or when she took the new book from the library into a room by herself and passed her fingers over the lettering on the cover and felt a delicious guilt as she opened the pages and read the words inside – as if even reading might soil the thick, satin-smooth paper.

She thought of them, and sometimes she imagined that they were her special friends, whom she was going to meet. They made her feel glad; they made her feel wanted. But as the day of the concert approached, the words set up a clatter in her mind – an uncontrollable clatter. Sometimes she really did not know any longer what they meant. Then she would stumble, even with something so much her own, and mix them up. She would feel dizzy; she would not be able to look at anything without her eyes hurting.

"Why don't you let us hear your part, Gabriele," Lise said. "You can use us for practice." But Gabriele shook her head, and could not explain that she had to do this by herself – or not at all.

As the time drew near, the words touched her mind like the shock of blankets on a cold winter night. She wished that she did not have anything to do at all, like Jason. Jason was going to sing a song with his class, but that was nothing. He did not even need a costume, just his Sunday clothes.

They Had No Feeling At All

A rope was stretched across the platform in the gymnasium. Bed sheets were draped over the rope for a curtain. In the low cold cement passageway behind the stage, waiting their turn, the children were strangely quiet. If anyone giggled now, it seemed forced.

It was a quarter before ten in the morning, and the audience had straggled in, in groups of two and four, from home, from work, until, all packed in, they constituted a formidable array. The chairs had gone fifteen minutes before show time, then the floor in front of the chairs, then the space along the two walls and in back.

There was a buzz of anticipation all around. As this little group and that little group came out, necks craned and cameras clicked. These children – singing their songs, dancing their dances – seemed younger than anyone in the audience had ever been; they were older, the people in the audience, than these children would ever be.

Gabriele was almost unconscious of what was going on about her. There was no comfort in anyone or anything near. It was worse than being sick. Then the other faces were outside your pain, but when they smiled at you the pain softened. Now she was absolutely alone. The children around her – her classmates – she was sure now she would never really like any of them. The people outside the curtain – with the noise of their conversation and their laughter – could not hide the cruel nature of their reason for being there. They were there for one reason – to see her make a fool of herself.

The words, her words, felt frozen. They had no feeling at all.

She tried to think of yesterday, then the day before yesterday, then the day before the day before yesterday. Far enough back in time was a place where she had felt safe.

She pictured the baby Jesus in the manger. He was safe. His Father in Heaven looked after Him. God never died or went away. Jesus had no reason to fear. He would always be safe.

She pictured Jesus on the cross. He was still safe, in his heart. "Father, why hast Thou forsaken me," He cried out. But He still knew, in His heart, that His Father was there, watching, caring.

She remembered the cross her mother had fixed to the wall above her bed, and the time she had explained what it meant. Even when her mother could not go to the Catholic church, because it was too far away, she never stopped being a Catholic. If Clara went to the Methodist church, it was because it was Clinton's church and because she wanted her children to have a Christian up bringing. But she never did come to like the Methodist church, because of its strictness: everything had to be thought through, and in such clear, cold, bloodless language.

She remembered the night her mother died – the night Christopher, her brother, did not want her to go in because, he said, "She's too tired, she has to rest." But when she called Gabriele's name, he didn't say anything but let her go in.

Every night Clara wanted Gabriele to sit with her awhile and keep her company. Sometimes Gabriele would get under the covers with her and they would talk. Sometimes all Clara wanted was to hold Gabriele's hand. "Otherwise," she said, "I might never be able to feel

God's presence again." When she felt an attack of pain coming on, she tried to pray, but there was never any relief anymore. Only when she was holding Gabriele's hand did she feel any relief.

Once, half asleep, forgetting that Gabriele was in bed next to her, she had let out such a long, unearthly moan, the pain was so great. Then, too late, she remembered the child in bed beside her; afraid of the harm she might have done, she willed herself to be quiet.

"Why is God so mean?" Gabriele asked.

"God is not mean," Clara answered. "It's just that sometimes we don't understand His ways."

"If God is not mean, why does it hurt you so bad?"

"It's a kind of test, I think. I must first pass this sentence of death on everything having to do with this life, even my health, my enjoyments, my children, even to know myself, everything, dead to me, and myself, dead to them. Then to trust in God through Christ, that in the world-to-come all these things will be restored to me, but in a new way. Poor child, you must be left alone, you must suffer hunger, cold, nakedness, though I cannot endure that the wind should blow upon you. But yet I must venture you as well, you above all, with God, though it pains me more than this pain to have to leave you."

She remembered as well the day Christopher came back from the city, where Clara was in hospital, and got angry at Clinton because he was drinking all the time. Clinton would not go into the city to the hospital to see Clara, because he was afraid. Christopher called him terrible names and said he had to stop drinking, because it was up to him now to look after Gabriele. Clinton laughed. "Oh me and Gabby, we understand one another," he said, and looked at Gabriele for support, but Gabriele looked at Christopher instead. Clinton said a bad word, and Christopher went away.

"Why can't you take me, next time you go?" Gabriele said to Christopher one day.

"Too many people around," Christopher said. "And she gets so tired."

"When will she not get so tired?"

"Soon, real soon."

She had heard this same answer already, many times, and she no longer believed it. She used to believe it. She wanted to believe it.

Clinton had screwed up his courage enough to ask, when Gabriele went out: "Well, how is she then?"

"She can sit up; she can eat some, though she's often sick."

"And what does that city doctor say?"

"He says they won't be able to tell nothin'till next week. That's when they'll know for sure."

"She can lick it, I know that for a fact," Clinton said, and put down his can of beer hard on the table, spilling some.

"You'll have to go and see her next week," Christopher said. "She may not last much longer."

"I hope she'll be home by that time."

"If she's not, then you must come."

"I dunno."

"I tell you, it's not a question whether you want to. So you can just quit mopin'."

"What about Gabby? Don't you think she'll want to come along too?"

"She can come along if she wants to."

And Gabriele remembered another time, when Clinton was sitting in the arm chair in front of the television, looking up at her, and almost shouting: "There's no way to solve these problems except Jesus!" But she had no idea what problems he was talking about.

And when it was her turn to say her words, she remembered Christopher standing in the doorway of the kitchen, calling her to come in. He was leaning forward, with his arms straight out to the sides, to brace himself, to keep himself from falling, and she remembered thinking, that's how Jesus must have looked, on the cross, when He said, "Father, Abba, why has Thou forsaken me?"

She stood as if frozen on the high hot silent stage, not even daring to look down. She knew everyone was looking at her, waiting for her to say something, but all she could see was a many-coloured blur, that would not go away. Then when the class began to sing, she could feel the focus of attention shift away from her, and the hot burning sensation spread from her face into her shoulders and arms. Turning, she tripped over the hem of her costume, and almost fell, fleeing the stage.

She sat on a step, her head down, between her knees, her hands laced behind and pulling her head even further down. She sat completely still, as if turned to stone. Lise went backstage to talk with the teacher. It would be a good idea, they agreed, if Gabriele went home, instead of returning to her classroom with the other children. Gabriele, however, would not listen to anything or anybody. She did not even hear what they said.

When all the other children had returned to their classrooms, and there was no one in the gym except the janitor putting away the folding wooden chairs, she got up and followed Lise outside to the car. Alden sat behind the wheel, and he saw right away that it would be useless to say anything.

That evening it began to snow, and the snow fell all night, lightly; and the next day, when the sun came out, everything was white, and new again, and the street was alive as it had not been for months with children calling back and forth, and playing, and laughing. But Gabriele stayed upstairs in her room, and she did not come down to join in. She did not come down to eat breakfast, and she did not come down to watch television.

"Go away," she said, when Alden knocked for the third or fourth time, asking if she was all right.

It was no use. When Jason hurt himself or was sick, he'd let himself be comforted. He'd let himself be held. Gabriele only turned away, only grew more distant. In her remoteness was a sting that could hurt and humble.

Standing outside her door, with no way in, Alden began to question himself. What was he doing here? Where did he belong? Who was he? What did he want? He had believed that life could go on as usual, but life could not go on as usual. Gabriele was in trouble. But she did not want help. Perhaps she did not even want love.

She needed so much to know that she was loved. Yet how was she to know this, if she could not trust anyone? Was there any reason in the world why she should trust him, or Lise, when so many others had already failed her? He had hoped that with daily acts of kindness and thoughtfulness he would win her over, but this was beginning to seem less likely.

He wondered what was to become of the child. Her future seemed so uncertain. And because he loved her, so did his.

A Dinner Party

Alden rang the captain's bell over the mantelpiece, calling everyone to dinner. The children brought their glasses of juice, the grown-ups their glasses of wine or water. They all sat down in a flurry of excitement. The children hurried their way fussily through small portions, then begged to be excused, to run upstairs and play. They were more interested in the dessert that was to come than in the full holiday menu Alden and Lise had put together with so much attention to detail.

The quiet that followed the children's departure, coupled with easier access to the wine, brought the grown-ups, thus far a little subdued, to life. Elizabeth knew all the gossip at the School of Architecture, where she had a part-time teaching job. Lesley had kind words to say about the current production at Neptune Theatre, John Wood's *Hamlet*, though he thought the music, while eerie and effective in its own way, was "overcooked." Lise spoke about the many headaches they were suffering at the university due to lack of funding. "Class size is impossible," she said. "You might as well give up trying to know your students."

"Politicians are a bunch of assholes," Jane said, and everyone nodded solemnly.

Sabrina's squeals of guilty laughter were the first warning that something untoward was happening up above. Alden told Jane, who was about to rise, to stay, and he ran up the stairs to find the children in the bathroom, "playing boats" (as Jason called it) at the sink, with the faucet wide open, and water pouring over the rounded lip of the sink to the floor like hot, thin, pinkish lava from a volcano. The three children, pretending surprise, stood there without even the brains (or the inclination) to turn the faucet off. With a few sharp words Alden chased them away, and moved quickly to limit the damage. He was shaking too badly to deal with the kids, so he summoned Lise and went back downstairs.

Almost immediately, before he really had a chance to calm down, Elizabeth brought up the subject of his writing. Was it true he was working on a play, since coming home from hospital? Did it draw on his experience of having a heart attack? When could she see it? When would it be ready to go into production?

"After a long eight or nine months," Alden said, "I'm glad to be able to report that the torture, self-inflicted admittedly, has almost but not quite come to an end."

"A difficult birth," Lesley prompted.

"The first time is always h-h-harder," Elizabeth said, trying to be helpful.

"Only a fool would try it if he knew how hard," Alden said.

"Oh, I think you w-w-would," Elizabeth said.

"So," Lesley said, scowling, "what's it all about?"

"Yes, please," Jane said, sitting up, tickled pink to see Alden squirm. "Tell us about it, don't be shy."

"I don't think so ..."

"Oh, yes, you m-m-must."

"Well …" Alden didn't know how to say n-n-no to Elizabeth. "If you insist …"

"I d-d-do."

He took a sip of wine to steady himself. "Three single fathers meet once a week at the local YWCA, where their children, ages three to five, are enrolled in a class for new parents. The idea is that the parent, male or female, is supposed to stay and 'interact' with his or her child. What happens, though, is that the three single fathers (the only men present) sit and talk, and pay precious little attention to their offspring. One is a lawyer, one drives a taxi, one is out of work, on welfare. They talk about their problems, their worries, their anger. Each week they have some new horror story to tell. The guy on welfare can't get any money from the government for support: he has to go cap in hand to the food bank. The taxi driver doesn't trust his babysitter: he suspects she's fooling around with his little boy, though he can't be sure. The lawyer can't wait till his ex-wife drops dead: not only does she leave the kid for him to raise (and that already costs a bundle), she also demands support payments every month for herself, while she's already living with another man. The three fathers don't ever resolve anything, but they share their feelings. They find out they are not alone."

Dead silence followed Alden's précis. Was that all? Did that take eight months, or nine? Lise, standing in the doorway behind Alden (having come back downstairs from scolding the children), blushed and shook her head. Don't blame me, she seemed to say.

"Any comments?" Alden finally ventured. "I can take it."

"It's difficult to know what to think," Lesley said. "It seems so – superficial. A little, what should I say, self-indulgent. But perhaps," he shrugged, "that's just my basic argument against the modern theatre."

"No no," Alden said. "I'm sure you're right."

"I don't want to discourage you, God knows. Go ahead, get it produced. Let the connoisseurs have their innocent pleasure. We're all friends here."

This shut everyone up until Lise, taking a deep breath, asked if anyone wanted coffee.

Lesley said yes, Jane said yes, Elizabeth said no. Lise looked at Alden, and when he just sat there, without moving, she winked. As if waking from a deep sleep, Alden stood up, sniffed the air, and went out of the room, along the hallway to the kitchen.

Lise led the others into the living room. Lesley claimed one end of the long white sofa, and Jane sat down next to him. Elizabeth preferred to sit alone in the big leather armchair. Lise put a sheepskin on the piano bench for herself.

"They're very quiet, Lise," Elizabeth said. "What do you do, b-b-beat them up?"

Lise took the question seriously. "Sometimes I give the children a slap on the back of the legs if things get really out of hand. Not to hurt them, but to show them I'm not fooling." Jane said she was totally opposed to striking children at all. Lesley said he thought a good beating never did anyone any harm. Jane laughed, but Lise, aroused, seemed ready to move to the attack.

"You were beaten when you were a kid?" she asked.

Lesley hesitated before admitting, "Yes, and I had it coming too." He wrinkled his high round forehead, a sure sign that he was pleased with the way things were going: in this instance because now he – because of his confession – had become the focal point.

"And you don't think it did you any harm? I don't believe it."

Lesley stretched his legs, as if getting ready to get up and go for a walk. "No harm done at all." He tapped himself on the side of the head, with the heel of his hand, his fingers curled back and away. "After all, here I am."

Lise grimaced. "For example, you never had any problem making out with women?"

Lesley sat up. "Oh yes," he said, after a moment's reflection. "Elizabeth will testify to that."

But Elizabeth said to Lise, "Lesley likes to tell f-f-funny stories about his sexual f-f-failures." And at this she burst out laughing. But then, embarrassed, the laugh turned into a fit of coughing.

"Past, I'm sure," Jane said.

"Of course," Elizabeth said, choking.

Lise sat forward to catch Lesley's full attention. "How can you be sure your problems were not caused by being beaten as a child?"

Lesley spoke very quickly, excited and angry at the same time. "There will always be problems between men and women and we all suffer in some way. I guess your father never spanked you when you were a kid, but does that mean you never have hang-ups with men?"

Jane shifted her weight on the sofa, bringing one foot up and tucking it close to the buttock: "I was only hit once as a kid, and do you know why that was? I was twelve. We were sitting at the supper table, and my mother was lecturing me about sex. You know, how if I let some boy slip it to me, my whole life would be ruined. Like sex was some really awful, dirty thing. Nothing good about it. I put my knife and fork down and waited until she was done. Then I looked at her and said, 'I bet you and Dad still do it.' I wanted to see the look in her eyes, but my father reached across the table and slapped me in the face. He told me I was a slut and sent me to my room."

Lesley shook his head. Elizabeth asked if she could help with the dishes. "No," Lise said, more sharply than necessary. "They're still soaking."

Alden came into the room, bearing a tray with four cups of coffee, a bowl of sugar, a small pitcher of milk, and spoons.

"Did you hear the children," Elizabeth said. "It sounded like s-s-singing."

"That wasn't singing: that was praying."

"P-P-Praying?"

"I've been teaching them the Lord's Prayer."

Lesley groaned, and Alden looked around at him with some combination of surprise and anger in his eyes.

"I didn't know you were a Christian," Jane said.

Alden sank back into the chair. "I'm not, exactly …" He could feel the hackles being raised all around, and he didn't want to get into that kind of discussion.

"Well …?"

"I've never been interested in church-going," Alden said, "but I've always thought the children should have a taste of it while they're young. They can make up their minds later. They can reject it, if they want to."

"But what's the point then?" Jane demanded.

"The point is that for now at least they're exposed to a coherent set of values that they can live by and also they have this whole collection of stories, really good stories, believable stories."

No one spoke so he went on. "They like the idea of God but I never know what it means to them. I guess it's a bit like the idea of Santa Claus, they believe it and they don't believe it. But this business of praying, that's different. It's not just an idea, it's something real, like music, which they get all wrapped up in. Praying for them is a continuation of their inner lives. They pray about what they hope for and what they're afraid of."

He addressed all this to Elizabeth who nodded as he spoke and stared back at him solemnly. Now that he had finished, he looked at each of the others in turn, waiting to be challenged. Lesley sat forwards, rubbing the side of his nose with a finger. *Stick it in, stick it in, you prick!*

"I don't see how it's going to hurt them, a bit of the old religion," Alden reiterated.

Everyone looked at Lise, but Lise shook her head, not wanting to be drawn into another argument.

Jane was cross with her because she would not speak her mind. "Oh, I know," she said, almost shouting, "you've been through all this a thousand times and you're bored to death with it."

Lise refused to be baited. "You seem to have all the answers," she said.

"Yes, you t-t-talk," Elizabeth said, her face tense, almost white, because of all the anger she felt building around them.

"I don't know," Jane began. "There are so many things that bother me about Christianity." She looked at Alden. "And since you don't really believe in it yourself, perhaps we should talk about that."

"Okay," Alden said. "Let's hear it."

"Well, for a start, the Bible is a book written by men, addressed to men, and picturing a very male God who even looks like a man because he made man in his own image. That sounds very suspicious to me ..."

"Wait a minute," Alden said.

"Next," Jane went on, "women get a pretty rotten deal in Christianity. The idea of original sin holds them to blame for everything in the world since the Garden of Eden. They are weak, unclean, condemned to bear children in pain as punishment for the failures of Eve. They are the temptresses who turn the minds of men away from God, as if women were more responsible for men's sexual feelings that the men themselves! In fact women only exist at all as a kind of divine afterthought ..."

"You can't impose your thinking on societies that existed thousands of years ago. Christianity expressed itself though available …"

Lise stood up, suddenly remembering that they had entirely forgot about dessert. She went to the stairs and called for the children to come down. Lesley disappeared into the bathroom. Elizabeth, startled by all the sudden movement, followed Lise into the kitchen. Jane and Alden, deprived of an audience, found that they had nothing more to say to each other.

Jane didn't eat her dessert (Lise had made an apple cake, powdered on top in the German style), but instead returned to the living room, alone, and started playing some Christmas songs at the piano. Elizabeth came back in, followed by the children, and Lise, and Lesley, and they all gathered around and joined in. Even Lesley got caught up in the spirit.

The children, though red-eyed with fatigue, said they never wanted to stop. "Just a few more minutes," they insisted. Jane said she'd play one more song and then it was time for bed. So they all chanted:

Wee Willie Winkie
Ran through the town
Upstairs and downstairs
In his nightgown
Rapping at the windows
Peeking through the locks
Are the children all in bed

*For now it's **nine** o'clock.*

Jane left with Sabrina and Lise went upstairs with Jason and Gabriele, and Lesley and Elizabeth found themselves alone in the long living room with their grumpy, drunken host, who had not a word left to say, to anybody, on any subject, whatsoever.

"I'm t-t-tired," Elizabeth said, which was enough to get Lesley up and on his feet. Alden went with them grumpily to the door. He waved as they drove off.

Where were the children, he wondered. Upstairs? Already in bed? Already asleep? He could not remember if he had said goodnight to them or not.

Did it even matter?

He helped himself to a brandy.

And Lise? Where was she? Why did she not come back downstairs? Had she fallen asleep with them?

Grabbing his coat, he fled the house, into the cold.

The Agent

*I*t was too dark to see his way behind St. Francis School, so he came around into view of the severe main building of Saint Mary's University, once the bastion of the Jesuits, but no longer. Whatever authority they'd once enjoyed was slipping away, here and everywhere. Which is a good thing, he thought.

All along Inglis it was quiet. The houses were large and set back at a comfortable distance. Soft lights glowed in the windows. He came to something called The Newfoundler, a sort of club, a block above Barrington. Inside he could hear music, clapping, and the buzz of a friendly crowd. Someone had once told him that this was the only place in town where anything close to the real thing was going on. He was about to go in when he looked and saw that he had forgot to remember to bring his billfold.

Crossing Barrington, at the bottom of Inglis, he almost ran into a car when he wasn't looking. "I should go back," he muttered to himself. "But to what?"

He tried to picture Annalisa but always, in his mind, she was somewhere else – in Cairo, in Munich, in Paris. He tried to picture Jason but saw only his back, sitting at his desk, doing his homework, with never a word to say. He tried to picture Gabriele but saw only the scared look in her eyes.

Inside the train station he heard the echo of his own voice when he called, "Where is everyone?" A glass door opened into a wide, carpeted hall that led up into the adjoining hotel. At the top of the ramp he stopped opposite a bank of telephones, just short of the reception desk, and for a moment he could not remember what he was doing there. He fumbled in the pocket of his jeans and found a dime. *Yes, it is here – an evil time, a mean time, let it roll!*

He dialled the first number that came into his head. It was the number of his agent, in Toronto. He let the phone ring seven times, then hung up. *Why is there no answer!* He remembered it was late, and the office would be closed.

He did not know the agent's home number so he called information. For a good minute he stood there motionless, staring at the good-looking girl at the reception desk, until Bruce's address, in Scarsborough, popped into his head: 62 Sandhurst Crescent.

"Who?" Bruce asked. He had just come in from a play, or a dinner, or a date, or all three, and he was in no mood to talk shop. He was irritated.

"Alden Oakes. Remember I sent you an outline of my play about single fathers."

"How come the fuck you're calling at this hour?"

"I've finished now, and I'd like you to have a look at it."

"You'd like me to what?"

"It's all about the contemporary state of sexual politics."

"The contemporary state of what?"

"Sexual politics."

"Jesus Christ."

"Do you want to see it, or don't you?"

"What?"

"I said, do you want me to send it off, or not?"

"Look, Alden, if that's really your name, this is not the time or the place. I mean, fucking headache." He moaned. "Where are you anyway? No, it doesn't matter. Look, you know our policy. Ship the shit and we'll take a look. I mean, a smell. I mean, a listen. Sorry, I don't mean to sound rude. I just got in, and I've got this unbelievable splitting fucking headache. Let me say this. We'll give it a sympathetic reading."

"Is that all?"

"What else do you want me to say?"

"You could ..."

"Listen, I gotta go."

"Yeah."

"So long, my friend."

"Piss ..."

"Keep on pluggin'."

"Off."

Roses Are Red

*F*ive dollars was enough for a small bag of popcorn, a small coke, and a box of rosebuds, which is what Jason came plodding down the aisle with, in the dark. Close behind, Gabriele, with her five dollars, had bought two out of three the same, but a kit-kat instead of rosebuds, to be different. During the movie they went back for another coke each, complaining the popcorn was too salty. All of this Alden readily agreed to, if it made them happy. Where things got out of control was after the movie, in the lobby, with Gabriele insisting in a loud, stubborn, angry voice that she had to have more money to buy another candy bar – and if he didn't give it to her, she wasn't ever going to go home. And to show she meant it, she stomped her seven-year-old foot.

"Let's just get out of here," Alden said, hot in the face because everyone was looking. "It's too crowded."

"Remember last Saturday, when Jason went with his stupid cub pack to the museum?"

"What of it?"

"And when he came home, he had a Mars bar, and he didn't let me have a bite because he's so mean?"

"And?"

"It's not fair."

"I don't see what that has to do with today."

"I'm not going. I hate it."

"You hate what?"

"I hate Jason. I hate you. I hate everybody."

"I'm not going to give you the money. You've had enough to eat. Now, let's go." He felt sick, as if rocked in the sea of the swelling crowd and the sizzling heat and the awful stench of buttered popcorn. "No more fooling around."

But Gabriele stood her ground in the middle of that mass exodus. She felt sick herself, sick of being knocked here and there, and she was determined to have her way. She would not move. All around her the carpet was littered with bits of popcorn and paper wrappers and soft drink cups. Alden took hold of her hand and pulled her against her will towards the door but she resisted. In her eyes was a look he had never seen before, frightened and furious at the same time. And before he knew it she was swinging at him, wildly, her hard little fists hitting his arms, his chest, his stomach. He held a hand up, to defend himself. She bit into the flashy heel of it, remembering too late that biting automatically meant two episodes of her favourite T.V. show.

He thought she had finished. Kneeling down, he wanted to hold her and tell her that all was forgiven, when, without warning, she hit him again, knocking his glasses off and causing one of the lenses to pop out. Shocked out of himself, he let go, and she ran off. Still on his knees, he cast around for the lost lens.

Strangers turned and looked, asking themselves (he had every reason to suspect) what this bearded man with the spiked hair had done to deserve such a swat in the face from such an obviously set-upon child. Was he a child molester? Should someone call the police?

He was wounded. Still, he had to get up and hurry after her because he was afraid that at her age she would not see the cars pulling out one after the other from the now snow-clogged parking lot beside the theatre. Or she might wander off. After all, he was responsible!

The event was ruthlessly hushed up. At home no one breathed a word about it to Lise, who remained in the dark. School started, and everyone hid behind the pillars of the daily grind. On the surface everything was back to normal. *It's just me. She doesn't like me for some reason. I probably remind her of someone she used to know.*

He resolved to keep a low profile for the time being.

*J*ason knew that Gabriele was having trouble adjusting, because she was so moody and difficult to get along with. He was patient but not endlessly patient. She could not expect special treatment all the time. If she was going to push him, he was going to push back. If she was going to demand things, he was going to demand things too. Every day there was something to disagree about, something to fight about. Who was to have first use of the bathroom in the morning. Who was to sit where at the breakfast table. Who was to watch his or her favourite T.V. show, when there was a conflict. Who was to be the first to confess having cheated at 'Monopoly.'

For his part Alden found himself more and more given to outbursts of rage, for which, when he thought about it, he could find no excuse. The children brought out a side of him he had not know before – a dark side, a hateful side. "Just put your foot down," Lise advised. "No display of emotion. Half the fun for them is seeing you explode."

He failed to understand what she was talking about. When the children fought he was sick in his stomach. One part of him knew that Lise was right; the other part continued to storm and rail.

The Sunday evening before Valentine's Day he worked with the children making cards to send out. After two hours of good, solid, spirited work, Jason, without provocation, wrote on the back of a card and slid it across the table to Gabriele when he thought no one was looking: "Roses are red, Violets are blue, The Sewer stinks, And so do you." Gabriele, in tears, fled the table. Jason enjoyed his triumph more than he missed having a story, a cup of hot chocolate, and a kind word before bed.

Such behaviour Alden had to admit in the end he could make no sense of. The conflict between the children was real – as real as a mountain gorge, an open elevator shaft, a damp basement. Any words he could find to explain the conflict were no more real than a puff of cloud on a hot summer day – beside the point, at best. He had only to say a phrase out loud, such as "When he sees that she's getting something that he doesn't have he feels jealous," and immediately the words dissolved, and his mind spawned images that had nothing to do with the words, so that the words seemed like small rafts bobbing about on an enormous sea of images. So he could no longer think at all – or speak. Or he could only think when he thought fast, very fast, without looking back at what he had thought, because when he looked back it was all nonsense and he had to stop. And so he gave up thinking and trying to understand and only tried to sympathize. I stand to be corrected, was his new philosophy. But the children did not want sympathy and they did not hesitate to label him, in their minds, a wimp. To prove this, whenever he stopped arguing and tried to sympathize, they stepped all over him, in tandem.

The Runaway

*T*he first time Gabriele ran away was Valentine's Day. It was a cold, windy day, and Alden had volunteered to pick her up after school. She said she would rather walk. "It only takes ten minutes," she said. "You think I'll get lost?"

Jason had very firm instructions to keep an eye on her and make sure she got home safely. As a rule he took this kind of responsibility seriously. He was mature beyond his age. He had done it before. So Alden was doubly surprised when he appeared at the front door with the news that he had lost Gabriele somewhere along the way and didn't know where she was.

His story was plausible enough. He had gone into a corner store to buy a pack of gum, and when he came back out, she was not there, where he had left her. Where she was supposed to be waiting for him. He retraced his steps to the school and searched the playground, but she was not there. He looked everywhere but could find no trace of her.

Fearing the worst, Alden called the police. He and Jason retraced Jason's steps to the store and to the school. Lise, alerted by Alden, left in the middle of a class at university and drove to the scene. She spotted her in the vacant playground of a day-care centre a block from the candy store, sitting in a swing, not moving. At her feet she had dumped and scattered her green and white plastic Sobey's bag of Valentine cards, one from each of her twenty or so classmates. But the one card she had really wanted, from a boy named Stephen, who lived on a farm across the road from her where she grew up and who she still considered to be her only friend, had not come. He didn't even go to her school.

The second time she ran away Alden and Lise began seriously to worry about the long-term implications. Lise tried to get her to talk about her parents. Did she miss her mother very much? Was she very close to her father? Did she worry about him, because he had such a problem with his drinking?

"Would you help me?" Lise said. "I really need to know."

Gabriele would not help her.

The third time she ran away Children's Aid was ready to move in. The child was not happy where she was. They would have to think about a different "situation" for her. Lise and Alden felt helpless, and a little bewildered. They cared for Gabriele very much and did not want to lose her. They had to agree, however, that it was not working out. She was getting worse not better. Their confidence in themselves, as parents, or substitute parents, had been shaken. Most of all, they feared for her future.

The father, Clinton, claimed, when interviewed, that he was working again, and what's more, he had stopped drinking. Upon hearing that Gabriele was having a hard time of it where she was, he began making noises to the effect that he wanted her back. "She belongs here, with me, not with them city people. She ain't used to no city."

He would, he vowed, cease drinking altogether, now and in the future – if they would let him have his girl back again. He loved her, he said, and only wanted what was best for her. If I don't get her back, he as much as said, I just might start drinking again.

Children's Aid, after some soul searching, came to the conclusion that they should not stand in the way of the child's return to her father, as long as he was able to look after her. They would stay with the case, naturally, until they were sure he was really on the road to recovery.

Clinton

*G*abriele sat glumly by the window, staring out. Clinton kept looking over at her, but she would not return his look. Stubborn as a mule, like always, he thought to himself. No change there.

The wipers on the van sloshed back and forth. "I guess you'll be glad to get home, eh?" he said, nodding. But when she shrugged her shoulders he said sharply, "Come on, cheer up. What is this, a funeral we're going to, or what?"

Out of fear and with a sense of pleading in her eyes, she looked at him now, like a little scared jackrabbit, ready to bolt. He was sorry he had spoken so sharply, but he couldn't stand it when she wouldn't say anything.

The rain beat against the glass. They road ahead was hard to see, beyond four or five car lengths. A truck passed them coming down a hill, and it was like having a very big bucket of water thrown in their faces. Clinton couldn't see a thing and had to slow way down.

The clouds were thick and dark over the basin, and the rain seemed to be coming down much more heavily out on the water. Sheer perpendicular sheets of it. Across the water the high ridge with its vertical drop-off, where the ferry to Saint John came in and out, was faintly visible in the darkness.

He hummed softly to himself, to fill the void that Gabriele's silence created in him. His weathered face was like the map of some faraway mountain region – patches of brown with two little icy-blue lakes that were his eyes. His voice was raspy, and quite tuneless.

"Going home, going home, the food will suit me-e-e. Going home, going home, I don't like the food in the city-y-y."

In her corner by the window Gabriele pretended not to hear.

The van climbed the last big hill before Clementsport. The basin fell away below, and got smaller instead of bigger, on account of the clouds. The rain let up, and a muffled silence settled over the entire shore. Everything was inert, motionless – only beads of water collected on the windshield, where he had rubbed the wax-soaked cloth. For the rest – along the highway, among the trees, over the fields – depth upon depth of grey cloud, grey mist, inertia, silence, and darkness.

This strip of shoreline was home to Clinton – or all he would ever know of home. His father, a carpenter, had worked at the army base outside Clementsport. His mother had died when he was three – "died" meaning, he learned many years later, that she had vanished one morning without a word and never been heard from again. Nevertheless, it had not been an unhappy childhood, as he recalled it. A child will laugh in the face of hardships that would drive many an adult to insanity or suicide. He did not think of them as hardships, only his lot in life. He had a degree of freedom that few city children could even dream about. No one ever told him when to go to bed or when to be home at night. No one ever told him to brush his teeth, wash his hands, or comb his hair. He was the kind of boy that respectable mothers warn their sons and their daughters against. A gypsy, like his mother, they whispered.

Clinton, like his father before him, was a skilled carpenter. He married a local girl, found land a few miles from the coast, outside the town of Elk River, and built his own house – a two-story, wood-frame house, which he painted white. He liked Elk River because it wasn't ugly like Cornwallis. And it was a prosperous little town, so there would be people who needed his particular skill. Clinton was a proud man in those days. He could do it all, he thought, and for a while he could. He gained a reputation as the best builder around. A number of houses owed their existence to his industry. He bought the only sawmill in town, which had been on the verge of bankruptcy, and restored it to health. Once, he ran for mayor (he was still only twenty-nine) and narrowly lost.

Things started to come apart for him when his wife died young, from lung cancer. He found himself, at thirty years of age, a widower, with two small children, and no clear idea how to raise them. Stubbornly, he refused to send them to relatives to be looked after. He would do it himself – the same way he had built up his business – with a lot of hard work, and never giving in.

Clara Huot, who was to be his second wife, was a teacher at the local school. She was a small, dark-haired woman with a great love of learning. Impressed by the degree of his involvement with his children, she overlooked his sometimes harsh treatment of them, which she herself was witness to. He was, in her mind, an "interesting" man – alive, driven. Above all, she liked the children, Christopher and Susan, both of whom she taught, in successive years.

After a brief courtship they were married. There followed an even briefer honeymoon. She learned the truth about Clinton: that he lacked any kind of fundamental trust in people and things, and that, as a consequence, he could tolerate no opposition at all, from man, woman, or child, once he had made up his mind. If the world itself, at bottom, was silence and nothingness, then people too, and things as well, at bottom, were silence and nothingness.

Gabriele was the joy of Clara's life. At the same time, having her was a rude awakening. She was forced to give up her job, with the further understanding that she need not waste her time re-applying for it after Gabriele was born, as only unmarried women would be considered for the position. When she made it clear that she intended to fight this unfair policy, Clinton turned against her, with demands that she "get rid of them fancy ideas" and stay home "where you belong" and look after "that kid." The rift between husband and wife was complete.

Even after she and Clinton were married, and Clinton's children were close to ten years of age (Christopher eleven and Susan nine), he continued to beat them, as if to tell her: "With your comin' ain't nothin'that's changed." "Just you wait and see," she said, but only to herself. "Things *have* changed; I *will see* that they change." To Clinton she said nothing, saving her strength for a future, decisive confrontation.

Christopher was always getting into fights at school. He stood up in class and said, "Fuck this and fuck that." He laughed at his teachers. He skipped school. He stole things. One day he stole money from his teacher. When Clinton found out about it, he didn't say anything but went into the woods at the back of the house and cut a new stick from the willow tree. He beat the boy as hard as he could but he wouldn't cry. Instead, he turned to him when it was all over and said, "When I grow up I'm going to be a self-respecting individual." Clinton locked him in a room in the attic and said to Clara, "He can damn well rot there, for all I care."

Clara had to take his meals to him on a tray and shove them under the door, which had a convenient three inch gap. He hardly ate anything. In these situations she felt powerless to act. If she ever stood up to him he started hitting her. The evening of the fourth day, with Christopher still locked in the attic, she smelled smoke. She ran upstairs and broke open the door. Somehow he had got hold of a book of matches and set fire to his bed.

When Clinton learned what he had done, something inside him snapped. His eyes flashed white – even Clara had never seen that maniacal look before. Grabbing the first thing he could find – the loose rung of a chair which he tore free – he went in to the boy and began hitting him over the shoulders and back until something broke. It was the rung. Clara came after him to stop him, but he pushed her away. He had twice his normal strength, which was already considerable.

Clara screamed and stormed at him, and Susan, behind her in the doorway, cried and howled, but he only stopped when Clara said she was going to call the police. He came at her, threatening her, but calmed down at the last moment. This happened not more than a year and a half after they were married. He beat Susan as well, when he was in the mood. Once he beat her because someone stole her bike while she was in a store shopping. Clara, who had sent her shopping, was not at home when this happened.

After this she would not let him come near her. She wanted to leave him but felt she must stay to protect the children. She told him that if he ever laid a hand on either of them again, she would call the police. She didn't care what happened to her. He threatened her and raised his hand to strike but never did hit her again after this, because he knew she would call the police. He would have to leave her alone or kill her.

When she had Gabriele, Clara was definitely finished with Clinton. He would have no role to play, as a father, where Gabriele was concerned. He shrunk a little, in stature. Christopher, and even Susan, found new strength to fight against his assertion of authority. For this too, he blamed Clara.

He wanted her dead, but when she died, several years later, he got no joy or satisfaction out of it. "She was too young to die the way she did," he said – and maybe he believed it.

Clara was forty-two years old when she died of lung cancer. At the end she insisted they bring her home. Gabriele was scared the day Christopher went to get her. Clinton opened the front door. He wanted to carry her indoors but he was too old. Christopher lifted her in his arms as if she were a child. Clinton had bought her a big, deep chair to put in the living room where her rocking chair used to be. When she was unwrapped and seated, and had drunk a little of the tea Clinton had made, she looked around the room.

"Don't think I don't like your place, Chris," she said, "but it's nice to be in my own home again."

Clinton, looking out from the kitchen, answered hoarsely, "It is, it is."

Gabriele came forward to be near her mother. "Why, there's my sunshine!" she cried, in tears. For a moment her eyes cleared and she was almost herself again. But a sort of devil possessed her and she began to cough again and she could not stop. She exhausted herself, until her face was all pinched with deep lines in the forehead and at the corners of the mouth. Her eyes were shut and tears came in more abundance, but not tears of joy, rather tears of despair.

Clinton was afraid of her now. He knew that she was dying, but he kept up an air of cheerfulness. Every morning he would go in to see her. (He slept now in Christopher's old room.) Sometimes he would help her into the living room, where she could sit and look out the window.

"Did you sleep well," he would ask.

"Yes," she would answer, with dark eyes, and he knew that she had lain awake.

"Has it been bad?"

"It hurt a bit, but nothin' to speak about."

He knew she wanted sympathy – but not from him. So he said nothing, and then it was as if the pain were his, as much as hers.

She was almost ashen, her eyes wide, all pupils, from the torture. Yet she would not weep or even complain much. Then her lungs gave out, and there came a terrible, dry cough, which seemed never to end, and then, what was worse, a suffocating shortness of breath.

She was suffering too much, Clinton said. They must get her to hospital. But Christopher would not allow it. "She has come home to die," he said.

He stayed by her side most days, and sometimes slept on the floor by her bed. Susan was often by her side as well. Clinton did not say anything more about it, but one night, when Christopher was away and Susan was asleep, he called the hospital and reported an emergency. She was spitting blood, he said. So they came and took her away.

Christopher almost killed his father when he found out about it, but Susan said it didn't matter any longer. They'd shot her so full of drugs she'd likely never regain consciousness.

"At least the children are grown up and on their own," Clinton said to anyone who came forward to offer condolences. Christopher lived in a house in the woods on the other side of town, where he had a girlfriend. Half the time he was gone to Ontario, working as a farmhand, or just looking for work. Susan, who had been away, in Halifax, attending university, quit her studies when Clara died and came home. With some money she'd saved she rented a house. She could not find work, so she set up her own day care centre, in the basement of the house. But Gabriele, who was not grown up, remained at home with Clinton. He had never thought much about

Gabriele while Clara was alive nor did he think much about her for weeks after she died.

Friends and Neighbours

*C*linton had, as promised, stopped drinking, but this was a double-edged sword. He was "responsible" now, to see to it that the child learn to tell right from wrong before it was "too late." The sweep of what might be counted as wrong behaviour was staggering. If she was a few minutes late getting home from a friend's house after school, this was wrong. If she forgot to do her homework as assigned, or made too many mistakes, this was wrong. If she missed the bus in the morning because she had overslept (even though it was Clinton who was supposed to wake her and get her on her way), this was wrong. If she dropped a dish while clearing the table after supper and it broke, this was wrong, a sign of a defective character.

Nothing she ever did was right. Only her mistakes, her fumblings, warranted his undivided attention. She had one great desire in her life – to stay out of the way of her father. To become so small that he wouldn't even see her. School was a safe place, and every day she was sad when it was over. She grabbed at every chance to accompany Edna, Stephen's mother, into town to do shopping. She spent as much time as she could, within the guidelines set by her father, at Stephen's house, which was on the same road as hers about a mile down.

All during lunch (that Saturday when she learned that Christopher was back) Gabriele was there but not there. She was not even listening to what the voices were saying to her, so after a while they stopped trying. The voices were like a low humming noise, not words – not words she recognized. She heard Edna's chair when she got up from the table, she heard Stephen scraping his fork on his plate, she heard Howard coughing between bites because his throat was dry from smoking – but she did not hear the words. The only words she heard were those that Amy had shouted in her ear, loud enough for anyone to hear who was standing close by: *The only reason I called is because Christopher told me to.*

Edna put something down on the table in front of her, a piece of pie, banana cream pie, with a crust of Graham crackers. It was the thinnest slice Howard had ever seen, and he laughed – maybe he thought it was one of Edna's jokes, or maybe he knew Gabriele would not touch even that amount. Gabriele didn't care for desserts, even when she had an appetite, unlike their boy, Stephen.

Stephen was almost as quiet as Gabriele at the table this Saturday noon, but he had his own reasons – he wanted to get back outside and finish some play he had begun before lunch. But when he got up to go outside, even though he put all his dishes in the sink as he was supposed to do, Edna called him back. "Ain't you forgetting what we agreed to?"

"I can do it tonight," he said in a tiny, faraway voice – almost a whine.

"We agreed," Edna went on, not to be deterred, "if I let you and Gabby go to the store before lunch, and play outside, then *after* lunch you'd work on that school project."

"I got all day tomorrow."

"That's what you said last weekend and *nothing* got done."

"I promise."

"I don't want no more promises. I want you to do like we agreed."

Stephen was embarrassed in front of his friend. A short, thin boy, not quite eight years old, he stood there, his head bent to one side as if he were sitting in a car with a very low roof. "Give me a break," he said.

Edna took a deep breath, as if finally fed up. "You give me a break," she said. "I'm tired of talking about this all the time."

"What does it matter if I do it tonight, or if I do it tomorrow?"

"It matters to me."

"Gabby and me ..."

"Gabby and me can just cut out the back talk," Edna looked at Gabriele, sitting across the table from her, to let her know that she did not mean her, "and run along and go and do what I told you."

Stephen kicked the leg of the chair. "Fug it," he said. With a glance at Gabriele he turned and marched out of the room, ran up the stairs to his room, and banged the door closed behind him.

Howard followed Stephen out of the room but not upstairs. (He hated these scenes and tried not to get involved.) Gabriele did the dishes. When Stephen still didn't come down, she went outside.

It was too hot, with the sun beating down, to ride her bike, so she went into the barn and sat on a box for a long time, in the stall with the horse, Lucy. Lucy was old now and very placid but still handsome, with her red-brown coat and her black mane and black shanks. Gabriele ate from a bag of potato chips she had bought at the store and hid in the barn, and she let Lucy lick and nibble her hand. She wished Stephen would hurry up and finish his stupid project (he was doing something on dragons) and come out so they could go play again. Maybe he would come to the beach with her when it was time. Though she was almost seven and a half years old she was not ashamed to have a boy for a friend. Stephen had always been her friend, and she knew he always would be. She could count on him, no matter what.

The barn was their favourite place to play. They would sit for hours in the loft, talking or inventing games. Their favourite game was something they called "airplanes." They pretended that the loft was the bay of a giant B-52 bomber. One by one they dropped stones the size of duck's eggs over the edge, shouting out "bombs away" and naming this or that schoolmate, or, when feeling especially bold, school teacher, whom they did not like or had heard bad or disgusting things about. Older kids, towards whom they felt nothing other than fear or awe or some combination thereof, were also not exempt, because they were safe here.

The only person she felt like bombing – hurting – today was Amy. Amy was a girl in her class, and she lived closer than anyone else but Gabriele didn't like playing with her very much because she always had to have things her way. It didn't make any sense, because Amy's mother, Janice, was so nice. Janice was Christopher's girlfriend. She lived on a farm along the road that started in back of Elk River and ended in a T-intersection with Howard's road, not two hundred yards from Howard's property. Janice and another woman, whose name was Bernice, had come up from the United States a few years ago, and found this piece of land, all abandoned and overgrown, with a house in terrible condition, and they had taken it and made it work.

The Farm they called it. Sometimes Christopher stayed with them but he and Bernice did not get along. He had a shack of his own in the woods on the other side of town, which was draughty and cold in winter and not as comfortable as The Farm, but it was his own. Janice sometimes stayed with him at the shack for days on end.

Gabriele hadn't seen Christopher since she had come home. Whenever Clinton called Janice, all she would say was that Christopher was in Ontario, "looking for work." Gabriele didn't know what to think. Sometimes she thought he must really have gone. Sometimes she thought for sure he was still around but didn't care about her anymore.

Gabriele and Stephen had just got back from the store in town that Saturday morning when Amy called. Gabriele knew she had her own phone, in her bedroom, and she could picture Amy sitting on the bed, with the same kind of snotty pinched little smile she always got when she knew something that somebody else didn't. "We're going to the beach this afternoon," she said, "if you want to come along."

"Maybe not," Gabriele said, which meant no.

"Suit yourself," Amy said.

"Me and Stevie …" she started to say.

Amy's interruption was as clear and sharp as a surgeon's knife. "The only reason I called is because Christopher told me to."

"Christopher?"

"He's back, didn't you know?"

"No."

"He said to call you and tell you."

"How come you didn't tell me before?"

"I'm telling you now."

"Maybe I will come."

"See, you can never make up your mind."

"Yes I can."

The news that Christopher was back unsettled Gabriele. The rest of the morning it was on her mind, but she could not really think about it, because she was playing with Stephen and then it was time for lunch. But now, in the barn, feeding Lucy the last bits from her bag of chips, she could finally think about Christopher, think about how good he had always been to her, think about how much she missed him. She was sure that he would never forget her, or abandon her, or let anything happen to her.

Amy

*T*he sky became more intensely blue as the day wore on. It was almost transparent, as if the sun were burning away all layers except the last, which had just a hint of yellow, like the mist from a squeeze of lemon. Christopher was sitting outside on the steps of the porch, drinking a beer, when Gabriele pedaled her bicycle up the driveway. Behind him, on the porch, blocking the screen door, Sammy, a black Labrador retriever, lay curled on his side as if in a private place that no one should disturb.

Christopher wore lightly tinted sunglasses in wire frames. His face was handsome and expressionless. He had a sharp-nosed, severe profile, but from the front the face was round and more forgiving except for the ridged brows. Close up he looked weathered, canny, almost old. Gabriele had forgotten how bad his teeth were. How one of the front teeth was dead and brown and overlapped the broken one next to it. Because of this his smile, while warm, was always half-given, half-withheld. "I've been thinkin' about you," he said.

Behind the house the big chestnut tree, to which the swing was roped, creaked. Christopher drummed the step next to him with his fingertips, inviting Gabriele to come and sit down, but she stared at his new leather boots and pretended not to notice. "So, how've you been?" he said.

"Okay I guess."

"Are they nice to you over there?"

Sammy suddenly raised his head, all eyes and ears. "Yes," Gabriele said, turning to see what was bothering Sammy. Behind the barn, by the edge of the garden, Janice was walking with a stranger, a woman, taking her on a tour of the property. When she saw Gabriele, she stopped, raised herself on tiptoes, and waved a greeting, as if from far away, across a mountain valley. Then just as brightly, with the same buoyancy in her step, she turned back to the stranger and continued her walk.

But Sammy was upset – jealous. He was standing now, straining forward, barking, wanting Janice to come back. "Down!" Christopher snapped, simply yet with authority. Sammy looked at him for one second, saw no alternative, and slowly, carefully flattened himself on the floor, even stretching out his hind legs behind him, the length of his otter-like tail.

Amy called through an upstairs window for Gabriele to come up. Gabriele put her bike down in the driveway and went up the porch stairs. Sammy, as if glued to the floor, watched her pass by, his eyes wet, sad, hurt.

In the kitchen Bernice was putting together the basket of food to take to the beach. "I can't talk now," she said, and as proof she raised one hand in which she held a small cutting knife – the handle a bright red plastic against the brown of her palm.

"I'm going upstairs," Gabriele said, and felt stupid because Bernice already knew where she was going, where she always went.

Bernice's smile was tight-lipped, enigmatic. It was as if she knew something that Gabriele would give anything to know, and one day, when it suited her, she might decide to tell her – or she might not. It depended upon – Gabriele had no idea what. "Well, go on then," was all she said now, but it was like a release, and Gabriele fled the kitchen and ran up the stairs to Amy's room.

Amy's door was open. On her knees by the side of her bed she was stuffing the last possible thing into her bag, for the beach: a portable radio, with detachable speakers. Gabriele sat in a chair by the window.

"Have you got your bathing suit?" Amy said.

"I'm wearing mine," Gabriele said.

"Me too," Amy said, and she pulled her jersey top up to show Gabriele.

Amy was a tall girl, and big-boned. Because of the way she did her hair, cut short and uneven at the ends, and because of the clothes she wore, baggy jeans and a variety of sweaters or jerseys, she appeared bigger than she was, even boyish. But Gabriele was thin, pale, brittle, with large, light-blue always-on-guard eyes, and long, thin, straw-coloured hair, which she wore in braids. She was not as tall as Amy but looked taller because of her slightness.

Outside the window a girl Gabriele had never seen before was sitting in a swing at the bottom of the chestnut tree. "That's Jenny," Amy explained. "I don't like her very much."

Jenny was the daughter of Charlotte, the stranger whom Janice was showing around The Farm. Charlotte was from Boston. She was spending a few days with Janice and Bernice before driving to the Tatamagouche, where she had rented a cabin for the summer. About half an hour before Gabriele's arrival, Jenny and Amy had had a fight of some sort. They were no longer on speaking terms. Gabriele found herself, for the drive to the beach, stuck between the two of them in the back seat of the car, for the all-too-obvious purpose of keeping the peace. Christopher, at the wheel, pointedly ignored the lot of them, while Janice made sporadic but futile stabs at conversation. Bernice, Charlotte, and Paul, Bernice's boy, followed in the pick-up.

I Don't Love Him

*I*t was five degrees colder at the beach than inland. The wind off the water was strong enough to counteract the warming effect of the sun. Though the beach was crowded, those hardy enough to accept the challenge of the chill waters could be counted on the fingers of one hand. The early supper, in these circumstances, was decided upon a lot earlier than planned.

Still in shirt and trousers, Bernice set off down the beach with Sammy by her side, towards a high, rust-red cliff that jutted out, like the beak of a bird. Christopher and Janice unfolded a pair of beach towels and stretched out in the sand. Paul took Charlotte with him and returned to the car, for a ball, which Amy had forgot. The three girls, in long jersey tops, played at the edge of the water, teasing the waves with their toes.

When Sammy came back without Bernice, they wondered where she was. The girls could not see her, nor could Charlotte. Perhaps she had climbed the rocks at the bottom of the cliff and continued along the adjacent beach. Paul, whom the girls had done their best to ignore, was glad to be called into some sort of action. A search!

But Gabriele was the first to see her. Some distance off shore, beyond the row of markers that set the limit to the lifeguard's responsibility, beyond even where the waves began to well up and take shape, in a tan bathing cap she bobbed up and down in the water – only the tightly wrapped head was visible. Slowly, with what looked like little effort, and no fear at all of the cold water, she drifted with the current, or with an underwater kick of her own, towards the middle of the beach, opposite where the girls played. When she saw Gabriele standing, looking out at her, and waving, she waved back then sank down again – all but the head. Charlotte called for Paul to come back, but he was already gone, onto the adjacent beach, and could not hear.

Amy and Jenny were busy building something in the sand, very near the line that marked the farthest wash of the water. Gabriele, on her hands and knees, began heaping up tons and tons of wet sand, for a castle she was going to build. Amy and Jenny were friends again, and didn't want Gabriele around. They looked at each other with sly, calculating looks. Amy, in a voice as cold as the water they dared not enter this late-spring day, said to Gabriele, "Go play with your friend, Stevanovitch, wherever he is. We don't want you here."

Gabriele didn't move. She didn't budge. She didn't say a word. She kept herself as still as the shell of a sea urchin on the beach when the waves come crashing in, only looking up from its work to see when the next wave was due.

"How can you stand that – that nimrod," Amy said.

"He's not so bad," Gabriele said loyally.

Amy threw a handful of mud halfway between herself and Gabriele. "I know, you love him."

Jenny had to suppress a fit of giggles at the mention of the forbidden word.

"I don't love him."

"Everybody knows you do."

115

"You're lying."

With a fierce, cross look, and without warning, Amy reached out and gave Gabriele a hard slap on the face with an open, wet, sand-encrusted hand. Gabriele, in a shock of tears, leaped up and ran off down the beach, towards the breakwater. Sammy, confused by the sudden change in the tone of the voices, barked and chased after Gabriele, hoping this was some new kind of game.

Towards the end of the beach, as she neared the breakwater, there was hardly anyone. Red- (where she had cried) and brown- (where the sand still stuck) faced, she slowed to a walk. Sammy found a clump of kelp that had just washed in, with the last wave. He took the slick, dull-brown ribbon in his teeth and began tossing it left and right, with the same motion he would have used if it had been a dead bird.

The tan bathing cap moved towards this same end of the beach. Gabriele waded through pools of warm, calm tidal water, and came at last to the chain of rocks that separated and protected the sand of the beach from the deep, swift, inland channel beyond. In the sea's soft salt-spray her tears dried.

Climbing on the green, slippery rocks, she surveyed the scene. The wind blew strong and cold. The water, split between beach and channel, turned rough, ugly, alien. Little brown bubbles of a different kind of seaweed bobbed just below the surface, between the rocks, where the water was sheltered.

What She Had Been Seeing All the Time

Gabriele was afraid when she was at home with Clinton. This man, her father, into whose care she had been thrust for the second time, was like a stranger to her, and she did not know what to expect. She had clung so closely to her mother while she was alive that now it was as if she were aware of him for the first time. He was a presence in her life, a solid, unavoidable presence, with all his shortcomings on full display, unchecked, for the first time.

There were times, perhaps, when they did get along. Sundays, when they sat together at the table in the kitchen and talked about what they wanted to do when summer came. School days, when she brought home drawings she had made, in bright red, yellow, and green crayons, and he taped them to the side of the fridge where he could see them when he sat down. Evenings, when they huddled together in front of the T.V., sharing a bowl of popcorn.

But then she would do something "wrong," and no matter how trivial she would have to pay. It was as if he were a different person. But he was really the same. He was only pretending to be something he wasn't, the other times. It was the pretending that frightened her the most because it was so false and easily reversed.

Maybe she would forget to empty her waste paper basket, as she was supposed to do every Tuesday when the garbage truck came. Maybe she would forget to bring home a notice from her teacher, about a class excursion that was being planned. Maybe she would forget to flush the toilet. Maybe she would stay for supper at Howard and Edna's house without asking. No matter, he would use it against her. Then her stomach would churn, her head would spin, and his loud, angry voice would turn her world upside down.

Then she would do something really "bad" – such as running away. She liked to play a game with Stephen, in which they hid in the woods and didn't come out until someone came and found them, usually Howard. She didn't want to go back, even after it was dark. Stephen always persuaded her, except once, when she ran away from him. Stephen went in to tell Howard, and Howard came looking, but it was too dark – they could not find her anywhere. Howard called the police. Clinton was furious. He was furious at Howard, for not calling him first. He was furious at Gabriele, for causing him such embarrassment.

How was he to teach her so that she would not forget? He had told her many times what dangers faced a girl that ran away – the cold, the loneliness, the beatings even to the point of death she would receive if some man got hold of her. Nothing he said, obviously, got through to her.

An insane idea came into his head. Without stopping to think it through, he dragged her outside to his van and tied her there, to a bench. He drew the curtains so no one could see inside. He left her there for three days and three nights, with no food and nothing but a bucket of water to slurp from. This was to show her what it would be like, if she really ran away.

The whole time she never cried once, or tried to call for help. Sporadically, she struggled with the rope, until she had rubbed her wrists raw. On the road, a few days later, Christopher, when he stopped to talk with her, saw the marks, and though he said nothing and asked no questions, he knew very well from his own experience what must have happened.

She stayed away from school a week because she did not want anyone to know. Clinton did not force her to go – perhaps he also feared what people might think.

It was June, the second to last week of June – the last week of classes before summer vacation. Friday, report cards would be handed out and school would be dismissed at ten. Thursday, children would stay home while teachers completed their grades. Wednesday was the last full day of classes, at which time all desks and lockers had to be cleaned out. Tuesday, after school, Gabriele's teacher called, to ask if Gabriele would be coming in, to collect her things. Clinton promised she would be there.

The bell rang at five before three. Gabriele was glad it was all over and no one had noticed the marks on her wrists. Or if they had, no one had said anything. She had told her teacher that she'd been sick, which seemed to satisfy her. It was the last day of school, so what difference did it make?

Gabriele gathered up her things – two plastic grocery bags stuffed with pencils, crayons, magic markers, scrap paper, construction paper, work books, show and tell projects in bits and pieces, gym shoes, rain boots, an old shirt for art class, and a lunch box that was the sure sign she was from the country – and fled the room, and the building. "Wait for me," she heard Stephen call out from the far end of the hallway, but nothing could hold her back from reaching the goal she had set for herself.

Children climbed aboard the waiting bus, too tired for more play, and wanting to claim a favourite seat for this final ride home. Other children, who lived close by, trudged along the highway, dragging their possessions after them in the dirt and the dust. The most energetic finally quit the playground and climbed aboard. The bus was full. Morris, the driver, came back along the aisle, counting bodies. When he was satisfied that everyone was present, he pulled the door closed, turned the key, and started away.

Gabriele and Stephen sat together, as they always did, but today was different. All day she had hardly said a word to him, and he did not know why. She had been out of school a week, during which time she had not once come over to his house to play. Several times he had seen her outside on the road in front of her house, riding her bicycle, but when he came out to play she went back inside. He did not know what was the matter with her. Maybe she's mad at me, he thought, trying to remember what he might have done.

Morris got off with them, as he always did, and shooed them safely across the highway. Stephen started up the dirt road towards home, towards summer, towards long lazy days, towards the luxury of no-school. Gabriele trailed behind, and even stopped and turned around and looked at the bus as it continued along the highway, as if that's where she wanted to be, not here on the dirt road on the way home.

"What's the matter with you today," Stephen said, coming back down.

"Nothin'."

"You wanna come over and play before supper?"

"Ain't supposed to."

"You go ask."

"Don't want to."

"He'll say yes, I'm sure."

"What do you know?"

"I'll be in the barn, okay?" He went on his way, towards home, swinging his bag in a wide circle above his head.

When Gabriele opened the screen door and stepped inside, she was glad for the cool air. Her face burned with the coolness. And the smell of something sweet: some kind of food. From another room came the sound of a woman's voice. It was monotonous – unreal. She was arguing with someone, in muffled tones. It was not her mother.

Gabriele stood in the entrance and instinctively looked around her. She saw a smear of blood on the floor.

A faint smear, which seemed to lead through the door into the room where the television was on.

The coolness of the house pitted her face. She came forward on legs that were suddenly elastic, after the long day at school when she was all clenched up inside, almost unable to move.

Someone was sitting in the chair in front of the T.V. Clinton. He did not look around when she came in. Or even move. It was a joke she thought. He was joking her. The way he sat slumped down in the chair, his head pushed forward into his chest – it was a joke.

"Daddy," she said, in the barest whisper. For a long time she had not called him Daddy.

"Daddy …?" His eyes were open. It was strange to see him sitting so still, with his eyes open, without moving or turning to look at her.

Her focus narrowed, and now she saw what she had been seeing all the time, since she had come into the house, since she had come back to live with him, since she had been born, without knowing it. Down the front of him there was blood – a cascade of blood, on his chest, on his stomach, in his lap, on the floor where his ankles were tucked in under the chair and crossed.

She stood next to the strange man, waiting for him to speak.

The blood smelled sweet; it smelled sticky. She wanted to throw up.

A cloud rose to her, blotching her sight.

The whimpering from the T.V. was sweet because it was so soft.

Outside, muffled in the distance, a dog was barking.

She stood there, for the longest time, unable to move, unable to think. Her face was hot in the welcome air of the house. Her brain had dissolved in the sweetness of the welcome.

She looked down at this dead body as if to figure it out. It had to be a joke.

She reached down, touching the shoulder. At the same time something made her look up.

She looked up, through the door, into the kitchen.

Her fingers burned. She was on fire.

He Dreamed He Met a Stranger

*A*t the top of the last hill leading into Clementsport Alden stopped the car and got out. Through the summer haze he could see across the water to the opening into the Bay of Fundy. An almost vertical cliff slanted down more brown than red in the dolphin blue border between sky and sea. A ribbon of highway wrapped the side of the hill above and into the ferry terminal. A scattering of buildings along the curve of the basin was the town of Digby. Closer to him was a green island with a white house nearly hidden in the massed trees.

In low gear he started down the hill. The road curved in and down, past a white clapboard church, starkly white because of the blue water behind. Farther down was an abandoned service station, the old pumps stripped away leaving the cement island and rusted stumps where the pumps had been. The woods behind and on either side of the abandoned station were thick, green, untouched, and alive.

At the bottom of the hill was a one-lane plank bridge, under which flowed, at low tide (as it was now), a trickle of water from the woods. Across the bridge, where the road curved around again before starting another steep climb, was a clump of old brick buildings, some two, some three stories high, all on one side: a post office, a drug store, a variety store, a bank, a locksmith, and a corner store. If any, or all, of these stores were still in business, there was no telling by the presence of customers coming or going. Farther along, between the highway and the bank of the estuary, on a strip of oiled gravel, was a second, functioning service station, with a coffee shop attached. Alden pulled in, next to the only pump.

The man who came out from the garage to work the pump was old, unsteady on his feet, but friendly. The boy who came out of the coffee shop to ask for a ride was young, pale, strange, with one arm twisted and bent out of shape, as if deformed. Over his shoulder he carried a canvas bag and on his head he wore a red and white bandana.

He looked in through the open passenger window. "Headin'my way," he said, in a funny, mocking sort of voice, more a statement than a question.

His canvas bag was big, bulky, and stuffed full. On top it had a flap that was tied down with a rope, through fat metal holes. With one end of the rope still wrapped around his hand he held the bag in his lap, with his arms crossed on top. He closed his eyes and took a deep breath. "Some fuckin' adventure," he said.

Alden paid the old man, and pulled out onto the highway. "Are you from around here," Alden asked.

"Not exactly."

"Where then, exactly?"

"Farm outside town." He looked at Alden. "I was visitin'my uncle over in New Glasgow. He said he'd have a job for me in the lumber mill. The job fell through, so I'm goin' home."

"Going home, going home. I know the feeling."

They drove along the side of a black, busy brook, into hilly, tree-rich country. They crossed a bridge and went up a long, low hill towards the top of which, beyond a little roadside cemetery, the road forked. "Which way?" Alden said.

With his elbow the boy jabbed at the window, indicating the right fork. In profile he had a hooked nose and full lips, and he looked much older than before. "What will you do with your summer? Now that the job's fallen through."

"Hang out downtown. Pick up girls. Ride around. Drink."

"And what do you do for fun?"

He mumbled of movies, going fishing, wishing he could drive to Montreal and talk to some people. Alden thought about this a moment. "What do you want out of life?" He was honestly curious.

His dark eyes surveyed Alden. "What the fuck you care."

His lot in life was fixed, his eyes said. The emptiness shaded into a kind of sadness that reached back generations in his blood from not having done what was crying to be done – whatever it was. Everyone knew what it was. Didn't they?

"Just asking," Alden said.

"Only thing I know is farming."

"Do you like farming?"

"Not much."

They started down a long straight stretch of road with several ups and downs, like a roller coaster. Alden felt sick in his stomach and slowed the car to a crawl.

"What about you?" the boy asked, his turn to probe and needle. "Where do you come from?"

"Halifax," Alden said, and when the boy seemed ready to lapse again into silence, he added, "I've come up for a funeral."

"Yeah, who?"

"Clinton Lockerby."

"I heard about it."

"Did you know him then?"

The boy laughed. "Sure I knew Clinton. Everyone knows everyone around here. It's a small town." He looked out the window, as if the town he was talking about was just coming into sight, around the bend.

Down one more short, sharp drop they charged, then past a garage, an autobody repair shop (a mountain of wrecked cars in the back), and beyond this a long, green, treeless hill on top of which perched a two-storey, burnt-yellow farmhouse and a barn with an aluminum roof, shiny new and steeply angled.

Alden pulled over and let the boy out. The name on the mailbox read "Harold Rafuse."

The boy came around the front of the car and stood by the mailbox, at the bottom of the driveway, as if positioning himself to have his picture taken. "Thanks for the ride," he said.

"Do you know a place in town I can stay?"

"Only place is Molly's down the road. Just follow the sign as you come into town."

"Thanks." Alden shifted gears and pulled away.

In the mirror the boy hoisted his bag onto one shoulder.

I Won't Hurt You

*L*osing Gabriele had hurt Alden in a way he did not yet understand. In the few short months she'd been with him he had grown very fond of her. There was no time at which he could say, "For the sake of *this* is all the rest." His love for Lise? He and Lise had long ago followed their own stars and drifted apart. Jason? Jason was growing up, entering into his own world – a world apart, a world in which he kept his own counsel. His writing? But he had come to a stand-still in his writing, and he was having trouble seeing where it was leading him, if anywhere. He no longer believed in himself, as a writer.

He existed but his existence had no centre. For a fleeting moment he had thought that Gabriele could be that centre. But Gabriele, if she was the centre of anything, was the centre of a storm, and like the eye of a storm, she had come and gone, leaving wreckage in her wake. Feverish, fuzzy-headed, without enthusiasm, he went back to Children's Aid, asking to look at some other possible names, but nothing seemed right. Nothing fit. This futility continued for weeks. But then, with Clinton's death, the possibility that she might be available to them became real again.

Might was the word that was emphasized in official channels. "She's been through so much," was the consensus, "we think it better to hold off a little before making a decision."

And?

"We did mention your name to her, and she seemed glad to hear it."

And?

"It wouldn't hurt to drive over there and have a talk with her. See what she thinks."

In the meantime?

"She's staying with neighbours."

Alden did not stop to think because thinking had nothing to do with it. Lise could not get away because of her job. It was decided that Alden would make the journey himself and report back. At ten that Friday morning he set out on the three-hour drive to Elk River.

*T*he road into town curved down yet another steep hill to an iron-black, metal bridge below. Halfway down the hill, just before the old brick school building, a road branched and ran parallel to the river. A sign pointed the way to Molly's Bed and Breakfast, which was a quarter of a mile from the highway.

Three stories high, the façade resembled a wedding cake, with an elaborate entrance decked with two dormers. To the right of the entrance, at the level of the second floor, there was an overhanging dormer window, with triple bell-cast roofs. There were two chimneys in the steep main roof, serving perhaps half a dozen fireplaces. Yellow, with brown trim, it was as if a house from Victorian Lunenburg had been picked up by a strong wind and set down on the outskirts of Elk River, across province.

Alden drove up the circular gravel driveway. Everything was quiet – the house, the yard, the hillside, the river below. At ground level, to one side of the main entrance, was a tall bay window, with the original wood, black-painted storm windows in place. In the middle of the yard, down from the bay window, stood an ancient apple tree in full flower. An uncut lilac hedge, running up from the road, separated the yard from the adjoining property, which was plain hillside. Behind the house, the land rose sharply into a field of tall, wild grass, with a forest of evergreens above this.

The door was standing open. Inside the little entrance way or mudroom was a pine chair, with a small rounded back, and above the chair four pegs on which to hang hats and coats. A red plastic umbrella stood in one corner. Black rainboots in another. He knocked on the inner door.

When there was no answer he tried the knob. Inside there was a uncarpeted hallway leading to the back of the house and a stairway, also uncarpeted and made of the same thick, yellow wood, leading to the second floor. A stained-glass window halfway up the stairs let in the sun. There was an uncluttered, spacious feeling because of the sun, and because of the richness of the wood.

Against an inner wall, opposite the stairway, was a hot-water radiator. On a table by the radiator was a vase of wildflowers and next to the vase, propped up, an unopened envelope. Alden looked at the name on the envelope.

The quiet was broken by a gurgling sort of growl that Alden had trouble placing at first but then saw belonged to a cat, perched on a stair above him, within arm's reach through the open rail. It was such a soft, almost inaudible growl that it seemed initially to suggest not genuine anger but make believe, as an actor might practise before a

The Baptism of Alden Oakes

mirror the emotion of anger. But the look in its eyes told a different story.

It was a big cat, all white, with bold, yellow eyes. With its four paws hidden somewhere under its large body, and with its head tucked in, it had shaped itself into a ball, but a ball that seemed set to spring, at a moment's notice.

Alden reached out and put his hand slowly between the rails of the banister. Without moving another muscle of its body, the cat opened its mouth and let out a long, loud hiss of warning, showing long, yellow teeth. Its breath smelled like scorched bacon.

"I won't hurt you," Alden said, softly. At the sound of his voice, the cat fled up the stairway, on quick, strong legs, and disappeared into the darkness.

*M*olly was not her real name. Her real name was Hattie but she thought Hattie sounded too harsh, she said. She was sixty-eight years old, short, white-haired, with a small dry face and eyes that smiled. Her glasses hung from a black, elastic cord around her neck. She had a bad hip (from a fall, she volunteered), which gave her a pronounced limp when she walked. Alden kept a polite distance behind – as if worried that she might at any moment repeat her fall – as she led him along the hallway into the kitchen and up a narrow back stairway.

"You won't mind sharing a bath," she said, stopping at the door to number twelve. It was more a statement than a question.

"Not at all."

"Anyway, there's just you and one other couple. They're from Quebec. I believe the man speaks English."

Alden went across to the window and looked out. The view opened onto the field behind the house. By the window was a small, oval pine table, on top of which stood an old, green, narrow-neck glass bottle, into which a bouquet of blue violets was stuffed.

"I'm sure you'll be very comfortable," Hattie said from the doorway.

"Oh yes," Alden said, turning back.

"Breakfast is served between eight and nine. There's coffee in the kitchen anytime you feel like it."

"I don't know how long I'll be staying. A few days."

"Whatever suits you."

Hattie went back down the same steep, narrow stairway they had come up.

Three Strange Creatures

*T*he bathroom, at the top of the front stairway, was newly renovated, in cheerful, bright colours. The sink was a large, old-fashioned catch-all with a small mirror above, in a pinewood frame. The tub was painted rust-red on the outside, white within, and stood on claw feet. The walls were light green, like mint ice that's begun to melt. The floor was nine-inch grooved pinewood, with assorted mats. The toilet seat and the tank were wrapped in pink terrycloth.

He felt clean again after his bath, and more relaxed than he had been all day. He looked around the room, his room. It was a small room but pleasant because of the colours and the care taken with the furniture, the bedding, and the fixtures, which were a variation of those in the bathroom. The picture on the wall above the dresser showed a vase of white roses on a table with a yellow book. A pitcher and a bedpan topped the dresser. A towel hung from a rack on the inside of the door. The headboard of the narrow bed was made of iron. The mattress sagged in the middle. He put on a fresh shirt and went out.

It was late afternoon. He felt like walking before supper. At the bridge there was a greasy spoon that he decided to try later. On the other side of the bridge he came to a corner store, which doubled as a service station. In a corner of the lot some boys were playing pick-up hockey, with a green tennis ball. There was a flurry of activity, and some good-natured pushing and shoving for the ball.

The store was empty except for the girl at the cash register. She sat on a stool behind the counter, reading a Harlequin romance. She had a round, fat face, and red lips. She might have been fifteen, or she might have been twenty-two. Her face lacked definition.

Alden bought a piece of hard candy to suck on while he walked, paid the girl, and went out again. *A pity she can't be out among the boys, playing hockey, having fun, but I suppose it's too late for that. The Harlequin romance, the red lips, the fat about the hips.*

He followed the road along the river towards Digby. High up on the hill the gaudy house that was Molly's Bed and Breakfast rose up in a clearing in the woods. He felt like walking and walking and knew he could at this rate. For an hour he walked along the road. There were very few cars coming or going. The only sound he could hear was that of his own breathing. After a while, with a quickening of his pace, the sound became so immense that it didn't seem to be his breathing but the world's.

He climbed a hill, lay on his back, and listened to the silence. The rays of the sun bleached his bones.

*T*hree strange creatures, long, thin rabbit-like creatures with big ears, started from behind a bush and bounded away.

I could live here forever, or until I die. Nothing would happen, and every day would be the same as every other day. The anxiety that belonged to life in the city would slowly leave me. I would be a new man. I would no longer have such cravings – for food, sex, learning. If I were cut, the blood would no longer gush from me, but seep, and

*after a little seeping it would dry and heal. I would become smaller,
and harder, and drier. I would be dried out by the wind and the sun.*

On the hillside he dreamed that he met a stranger as he walked
on the highway and the stranger invited him to come home with him.
Supper was waiting for them when they arrived – a meal of soup and
pan-bread. All the while he ate, the youngest, a girl, sat on her
mother's lap staring at him. Though her mother whispered in her ear,
she would not take her eyes off this new person who had come into
her life. The two older children kept their eyes on their plates.

The mother asked Alden about his journey. "I met a man the
other day," he replied, "who told me that they shoot people they find
on their land."

The father shook his head. "I've never heard of that," he said.
"People must help each other, that's what I believe."

Alden allowed this remark to sink into his mind. *Do I believe in
helping people? I might help people, I might not. I never know until it
happens. I don't seem to have a belief, regarding the idea of help.
Perhaps I have no belief. Perhaps I am like this ground, stony and
hard.*

It was already quite cool when Alden woke from his dream. The
sun had disappeared behind a hill. He was very hungry. But he
understood now, in some way, that this hunger of his had nothing to
do with real food, and everything to do with a lack of belief, an
absence of conviction, an emptiness that he felt in himself, and in
things.

The Funeral

*W*hen it came down to it he did mind that the mattress sagged in the middle. For several hours he was unable to sleep, until he taught himself to lie still, flat on his back, in the very middle, legs drawn up, head tipped forward with a second pillow below, arms crossed one on top of the other, hands on breasts. Then he slept soundly until seven thirty, when he woke to the smell of coffee brewing below.

The window looked onto the field of uncut grass. The sun lit up the spruce trees on the hill above the field, while the field itself, from the window to the fence, remained in shadow. A heap of a dozen or so discarded automobile tires lay in the tall, wet grass, near a shed.

The dining room was at the back of the house, behind the living room. The round table was set for four people. Alden stood behind the only chair that was not in direct sunlight. A radio played in the kitchen. He studied the picture on the wall above the buffet, which showed a tall ship at full sail, moving towards a green hill on which could be seen the few scattered buildings of a military settlement.

The noise of an electric mixer drowned out the music. Hattie came in with a small, carved-glass pitcher which she said was coffee cream, distinguishing it from the large, plain-glass pitcher on the table, which was two percent milk. Another pitcher contained orange juice. "I'm making waffles today," she announced. "Do you like waffles?"

"I love waffles," Alden said, though he couldn't remember the last time he'd had any.

The noise of the mixer ceased. "Good," she said, and disappeared into the kitchen again.

Hattie's other guests were late coming down. Alden stood in the window with a cup of coffee. The sun was beginning to move across the field of grass, from top to bottom. A dozen or so birch trees shone in the depths of the evergreen forest. A black and white dog ran around the corner of the shed. Hattie brought in the first plate of waffles, along with a cutting board with slices of bread, cheese, and smoked salmon. Alden took his place at the table.

He could hear their footsteps in the hallway above the dining room. Hattie returned with a bowl of scrambled eggs, a plate of breakfast sausages, and a tin of muffins. Butter, salt, pepper, various jams and honey circled on the lazy-susan.

Hattie poured herself a cup of coffee and sat with him while they waited. She wanted to know everything. Where he was from. What he did. Why he was here. She was like a digger digging.

He said he'd come up to attend Clinton's funeral.

She set her glasses on her nose and looked at him closely. "Did you know him?"

He explained his relation to Gabriele, and she laughed. "Well well, fancy that."

"Tell me about Clinton," Alden said.

"Didn't know Clinton well at all. A very private man. Never had much to say."

"You must have known him a little."

Hattie recalled the last time she'd seen Clinton. He was coming out of a store in town, drinking from a bottle of Coke. She remembered what he said: "This stuff ain't half bad, you know." She didn't say anything because he didn't seem to be talking to her.

Very quietly the couple from Quebec slipped into the room. The man, in a black turtleneck, sat down in the chair by the window, while the woman came around and took the last remaining place, across the table from Alden. The man, still half asleep, nodded and said nothing. "Bonjour," the dark-eyed woman said. "Very hot, n' est-ce pas?"

"It's been like this for a week," Hattie said.

"In the book they made us believe we would get cool," the man said.

"It'll be cool at the beach," Alden said.

"Oh no no," the woman said. "We don't like to swim."

Hattie recited the list of all she had prepared for breakfast, and mentioned the various kinds of cereal available in the kitchen, which she could bring out upon request. Alden helped himself to the scrambled eggs and a blueberry muffin. The man poured himself a cup of coffee. The woman contented herself with a bowl of blueberry yoghurt. Hattie went into the kitchen, to prepare another batch of waffles.

"This place is off the beaten track," Alden said. "How did you find it?"

"It's what I'd like to know," the woman said, looking at the man.

"I go by the book," the man said.

"See," the woman said. "He thinks he's smart."

Alden finished eating in silence, feeling awkward and as if he were somehow to blame for the awkwardness. The couple talked, in French, about their plans for the day, which included a stop in Wolfville on their way to Halifax, the reverse of Alden's journey. They wanted to see the parade of tall ships.

*F*rom a surfeit of food he went to a surfeit of wood, and again he felt that it was too much of a good thing. The church was halfway up the hill on the opposite side of the river. It was such a fine, well-made structure, it could have been the work of a schooner master craftsman of a hundred years ago. Outside, including the tall, square tower, it was made of cedar shakes, painted white with black trim at the corners and windows. Inside it was dark, varnished oakwood, which seemed softly to glow in the dark. The walls, with their small stained glass windows, the ceiling with its hammer-beam structure, the three-sided balcony with its "singing pew" for the choir, the triple-deck pulpit in the centre aisle, the high altar behind – everything was constructed of the same rich, deeply coloured oakwood. Impressively, it all seemed of a piece, like a ship. Alden felt carried aloft, into a luminous simplicity of conception.

The funeral was poorly attended. There were fewer than two dozen people, and half of these were women sitting alone, former friends of Clara's who had come not to pay any respect to the dead man but to remember Clara and support the children. The townspeople, because it was a well-known story how Clinton had mistreated Gabriele, mistreated all his children, were staying away in droves.

The children sat in the front row, opposite the closed coffin, Gabriele in the middle (only the top of her head visible above the back of the pew), Susan to her right, Christopher to her left. Christopher held his hand to his mouth, closed like a fist as if about to cough, and stared straight ahead, at the coffin in its gaudy ring of flowers. His high cheekbones and hooked nose gave him a primitive, aristocratic look, like one of the kings of Egypt.

Susan was everything Christopher was not – large, slow, friendly, inviting you with her friendliness, scaring you with her hugeness. Her short brown hair was so thin there seemed to be more scalp showing than hair, and she had small, darting, knowing eyes, under brows that were plucked bare. She had a permanent frown, even when laughing. With her lower jaw shoved slightly forward, she had a look that was vulnerable and defiant at the same time.

The bells rang out the hour. The minister came forward from the back of the church to begin the service. In the program he was listed as The Very Reverend Joseph Zinck. At the podium he shuffled a little stack of index cards under a pin light. He started to say something then stopped, unsure of his words. He looked at the three children, sitting squeezed together like sacrificial lambs, and he seemed to despair. Only Susan would return his look. But something clicked in his brain with that single look, and turning to the audience he began.

His talk focused on the all-encompassing, absolute gift of God's mercy, and the need "for we poor human beings to forgive one another, as our Father in heaven without favour forgives us." He reminded everyone of the "frailty" of the human animal. "It is not for us to judge, but for God." He rehearsed the significant events of Clinton's life. He offered words of comfort to those "still surviving."

"It is for these who are left behind, who must carry with them the grief and the sorrow, that we are truly gathered here," he concluded. The organist from his hiding place played "Rock of Ages" – Clinton's favourite hymn. The congregation was called upon to observe a moment of silence, to "think on" the deceased. Feet shuffled, eyes shifted, broken fingernails scratched bare places on the neck and the inner surface of the wrist. From somewhere towards the front a shoe tapped a steady rhythm, in three-four time.

A man in pressed suit and tie, with solemn face, appeared from the wings to announce that the service was over. "You may leave now and go to your cars." This was the funeral director, directing. Obediantly, everyone rose and began filing out of the side door to the parking lot. Everyone except Susan, who, alone apparently, had a mind of her own. Her eyes wet with tears, she stood by the casket in silent contemplation. As if in a conspiracy of silence, and in protest against the implacable machine that he himself was partly responsible for setting in motion, the Rev. Zinck came back and stood beside her, head bowed, Bible in hand. In a white heat of impatience, by the vacated podium, in the shadow of the pin light, stood the frowning director.

The cars had all been moved to a place near the side exit, to form a line in accordance with an unspoken rule of seniority, for the drive to the cemetery. The children of the deceased sat in a black car driven by an assistant to the funeral director. Friends of their mother followed. Alden was the last car in line.

The cemetery was a few miles outside town, on the side of a hill with a view of the river that gave the town its name. Rev. Zinck offered another prayer, then all were asked to join in the saying of the Lord's Prayer. Once this was done, with mixed results, the director again made himself conspicuous, like the host at a dinner party who gets ignored because the guests she's invited are so much cleverer than she. "The ceremony is now over; you may return to your cars."

But Susan, alone among them, remained behind, and would not be moved, would not be put through her paces like a dog, even if it was Clinton whom she had more reason to hate than to love. Mountainous in her loose summer dress, her thin hair blown almost to baldness, she searched among the flowers (brought by the bunch in the hearse with the coffin from the church and scattered about for effect) for one to remember her father by, before finally settling on a long-stemmed red rose that looked more plastic than real, as if it might last forever. She could not or would not throw the flower, or even a handful of dirt, into the open grave as the coffin was lowered into it (and as everyone else, not knowing what else to do, turned back and watched, as if this were the last and most important part of the ceremony), so she did the next best thing, she kept the flower as a momento to take away with her.

As long as she lingered there, no one else was going to go anywhere. Certainly not Gabriele, who only felt safe now with Susan.

And not Christopher, who seemed almost to welcome the chance to prolong the agony. And not Janice, Christopher's girl friend, who wandered, curious as a cat, among the more ancient of the tombstones, reading names. And not Edna, who stood behind the row of folding chairs and who, while not as massive as Susan, was as massively moved, knowing there was nothing she could do. And not Howard, who, while Edna remained rooted to the earth, prowled from the carside to the graveside and back again. And not Stephen, who sat inside the car, daring to look at a comic book he had stashed under the seat. And not Rev. Zinck, into whose hands all these who were the surviving had been entrusted, and who felt bound by this trust also to stick it out until the bitter end. And not Alden, the outsider, the intruder, who kept his distance and searched for his opening.

Reception

*T*he child sat on a log, digging her heels into the dirt. Her eyes were shut tight. "I'm sorry about your father," Alden said.

"I don't care," she said, raising her face to him, her eyes still closed, pinched tight, and making a face, showing her teeth.

Alden stood still, neither advancing nor retreating, as if she were a small animal which he had frightened. In her mauve dress, with a design in it of white flowers, and with her hair done up so tightly in two braids, sitting there on the log above the cemetery, she was the picture of abandonment. She was without protection in the world. He was suffused with longing: he would just as soon not exist in such a world.

A man may hold a child's hand. He moved a little closer, but she started up. "Don't," she cried, and he looked around, startled by her voice. By the graveside Edna was hugging Susan. Further up the hill everyone watched and waited.

"Maybe we can talk," Alden said.

Something in her eyes flashed and he wasn't sure if it was anger or some still deeper fear. "You're not my father. You never were."

He went down on his knees. "I love you. I'm not your father and I love you. Can you believe that?" He held her by the wrist and suddenly she was quiet, looking at him. He said, "Try to understand. You are, so important."

She stared back at him out of dark and unconscious eyes that seemed to spiral down and in, with a flash of silver at the very end.

He had a sense that he had come too late. She said, "I don't want ..." but she stopped, confused. He said again, "Maybe we can talk," and he meant not now, but some other time.

Susan called for Gabriele to come. Alden let go of her wrist, and she ran away.

To what does she fly? Nothing. And what do I have to offer her? Nothing. Or maybe ... .

He had something of value to offer, he knew. But he had to dig much deeper. He had to suffer. He had to go under.

First Rev. Zinck, then Susan, then everyone got into the cars for the journey back. What a relief for the funeral director, his assistants, and the diggers, for now, in the stillness of the freshly vacated hillside, they could bring up the oak casket, bring up the body in its bare box of pine, lift it out, set the casket aside, save it for future use, and lower the pine (roughly by winch) into the gaping hole again.

*A*fter the funeral there was a meal in the basement of the church. The basement hall doubled as a meeting place and a gymnasium. At one end there was a low stage of plank wood, at the other a basketball rim and glass board. Susan sat next to Gabriele on the edge of the stage, legs dangling, eating from a paper plate. Alden stood in line with a plate, a fork, and a knife.

Ahead of Alden in the line was the slender, well-dressed woman he had seen at the cemetery, in Christopher's company. Her name was Janice, he remembered. She kept turning and looking past him towards the door into the hallway, then turning back. She did not look at him or speak to him. Alden tried to think of something to say but could not.

Christopher had changed into faded jeans, brown work boots, and a white shirt with the sleeves rolled up. When he saw Janice in the line-up at the table he came forward, on bowed legs. "I feel like a man again," he said, frowning as if the worst were yet to come. The bones under the brows were ridged like the last obstacles a climber might face at the top of a mountain.

Janice said nothing but looked him up and down disapprovingly.

"Anything good to eat here?"

Janice shrugged. "The chicken looks good."

Alden felt dizzy. He almost dropped the plate he was holding. He had trouble standing up. Behind him, humming to himself, was an old man, perhaps seventy, with sunken cheeks. He did not know what to think. *Could this be Clinton's father?*

He had big, active, child-like eyes, and a raspy, barely audible voice. "You remember me," he said. "I was middleweight champion of Canada in nineteen hundred and thirty-three."

"What," Alden said, staggered by the claim.

"I was middleweight champion of Canada in nineteen hundred and thirty-three," the old man repeated in a loud, angry voice.

"That was before my time," Alden said.

"My name is Jones."

"I'm sorry."

The old man was disappointed. All he said was, "Oh." The spark in his voice was gone and Alden realized that somehow, in that brief moment, he had failed him.

He wheezed, then fell into a fit of coughing, which lasted half a minute. When the coughing subsided, he pointed to his throat, excused himself, and went in search of the men's room.

At the end of the table Christopher and Janice were unable to decide on dessert. "There's somethin' about apples," Christopher was saying, for everyone to hear, "that sounds, you know, healthier. You know, like fuck, *apple pie*."

"Don't talk nonsense," Janice said.

"I mean it. Maybe, just maybe, we're all fuckin' Americans with their apple pie and their guns."

"Just shut up."

"Mum's the word."

Janice looked around. "I bet there are just as many calories in that apple pie as in this banana cream pie, which I'm now, whether you like it or not, going to take a piece of."

"I have no doubt, little woman, that you're right again. As always."

"I'm glad you're finally coming around."

"I came around a long time ago."

*G*abriele moved her leg back and forth against the front of the stage. Susan, with a pat of her hand, indicated a place for Alden to sit down, next to her, on the opposite side from Gabriele. Even with his long frame his legs dangled and did not touch the floor.

"We've just been talking," Susan said. "We're trying to think about what comes next." Gabriele looked at him with her scared-rabbit eyes, to confirm what Susan said.

"I told her what you told me, how you' d love to have her come and stay with you again. Be part of the family."

"Yes," Alden said, leaning forward to look at her. "We hope you'll come back."

"She's not sure what she wants to do," Susan said. "She wants to think about it."

"So much has happened, I know."

"Why don't you two get together sometime and talk about it," Susan said.

"It's up to Gabriele," Alden said.

Gabriele shrugged her shoulders and said nothing.

"Okay?" Susan said. And then again, almost growling, in a teasing voice: "Okay?"

"Okay," Gabriele said in a tiny voice. She was not even listening to what they were saying but she was glad that it was settled, whatever it was.

"Where are you staying?"

Alden told her.

Susan nudged Gabriele. "What do you say?"

She looked at her sister, then at Alden. "Good-bye," she said.

Alden reached clumsily to take her hand. She slid from the stage and walked to the door, where she stopped, turned, and waited for Susan.

An Argument

*A*lden left his car where it was and started walking along the road below the church. H walked to where the river widened and emptied into the Annapolis Basin. The water was as blue as the sky, the only difference being that the sky was behind a thin haze conjured by the mid-day sun. He liked the feel of salt air on his skin. He left the road and climbed a hillside of daisies and buttercups. He lay down among the flowers and slept an hour in the sun.

It was after three when he got back to the bed and breadfast. Hattie was sitting in the front room with a new guest. In the bay window they were having tea and cookies. Suddenly Alden felt not sweaty-clean but sweaty-clammy; sweaty-smelly. He stopped in the doorway, bowed, and said, "Afternoon."

"Come over here," Hattie said, so dryly it was an order.

Alden came near but not too near, for fear he stank.

"This young woman has come all the way from Ontario to visit us." Hattie winked, whether on purpose or not Alden could not tell.

"Not too far I hope."

"She's a journalist."

"Freelance." She gave Alden her hand to be shaken. "Meredith."

"She's here to do a story on Digby. The decline and fall of. I guess that shouldn't be any too hard."

"Actually, I'm looking into the inshore fishery and Digby's my jumping off point, that's all." She stared at Alden with her green eyes, wondering if he might be part of the story she wanted to tell.

"I' d better get cleaned up," Alden said, at a loss for words.

He had no appetite for supper. He rested awhile then went out again, walking along the side road to the main road, and down the hill to the bridge. At the convenience store he bought a bottle of apple juice from the same girl. He wanted to ask her name and did she go to school, but was afraid she' d think he was hitting on her.

He hiked across the bridge and up the road to the white church. He sat on the steps of the church, taking sips of apple juice and watching the sun go down.

*L*ater, in the hallway outside his room, he overheard the couple from Quebec arguing. The wife wanted to start back in the morning because she was worried about their five-year-old daughter, who was staying with her sister in Montreal, who was "not in good shape" because her boyfriend had just moved out. The husband wanted to stay another day in Elk River before starting back. "I want to climb the mountain and I want to dig for clams," he yelled in English.

"I repeat myself, for the benefit of the hard-of-hearing," the wife said, also in English. "I spoke with Marie and she said *l' enfant pleur et pleur.* Now I ask you."

"You go by yourself. I'll go and climb the mountain alone."

"Now you are being difficult. *Difforme.*"

"Two lousy days without the child and you begin this whining, this breast-beating."

"What are you meaning to say? *Merde.*"

"Sssh."

151

"Sssh, he says. The child is maybe dying, and all he can say is 'sssh' ."

"*Il faut que tu n'as pas le sentiment exagéré tous les jours.*"

"*Tu ne comprends rien.*"

The wife stomped down the hallway to their room. The husband banged the door to the bathroom, his destination. The water in the pipe in the wall between the bathroom and Alden's room hummed.

His head back, his legs drawn up, his hands cupped over his ears, Alden did not move for a long time. And he did not sleep.

The Littlest Goalkeeper

*T*he rest of the house had been renovated but the kitchen was as old as it had ever been – the same old, heavy, oakwood caginets, the same old, chipped-porcelain sink, the same old, faded-yellow walls, the same old, faded-green linoleum, with its clover leaf pattern worn bare in spots but waxed and clean, the same old, out-of-date calendar on the wall by the window, with its picture of two calico cats pushing a soccer ball. The kitchen was Hattie's home, it was where she lived, where she felt real, and if this was so, then Alden found her conception of living very much to his liking. To keep, to maintain, that which is given you, that which is true ... to give, to bend, only so far ...

The kettle began to whistle. He dumped a spoonful of instant coffee into the cup and poured hot water on top. Added milk. In the just-grey window he took the first electric sip. Now he was awake. Hunger, which had gnawed at him towards dawn, had to relinguish its hold on him.

He carried the cup upstairs to his room. A noise in the doorway of the bathroom surprised him. The man who loved mountains was up as well, though it was barely six. In a yellow, terry-cloth robe, his hair sticking up every which way, he stood there, like a stunned cow. "Your bed too saggy too?" he whispered.

"Just in the middle," Alden whispered back.

"There is no middle for me."

"There's always the floor."

"I heard someone on the stairs. So it's you."

"I have few needs more urgent than coffee."

"Same for me." He put his finger to his lip. "Until soon then." He tip-toed back along the hall to his room.   Alden flipped off the hall light and went back inside his own room. He sat in a chair by the window reading a book until six thirty, when he heard Hattie stirring below.

The brief encounter with the man from Quebec seemed to have established some sort of bond between them. When they met again, at breakfast, they talked about their plans for the day and the weather forecast they' d both heard on the radio. They laughed when Alden said *je suis chaud* when he meant *j' ai chaud*. "I get hot just thinking about it," he meant to say.

His wife was just as amiable when she came down, ten minutes later. She loved Hattie's blueberry muffins, and insisted Hattie write down the recipe. Meredith was the last to appear, still in slippers, and sleepy-eyed. She had fluffy, mousse-brown hair. Because she took the chair at the end of the table, in the sun, there was as much red in the crown of her head as brown. Her features were small, almost muddied: brown eyes, a quiver of a nose, a pinch of a mouth that was painted red and that tended to curl up whenever she spoke. She confessed that as a rule she slept in. "I don't usually eat breakfast," she said. She sipped a cup of black coffee. It was as if the riches of the table, which Hattie had set out with such care, such pride, amounted to nothing, in her book.

The coffee woke her a little. On second thought she would have a piece of toast. She couldn't resist the sight of "that gorgeous honey."

"There's plenty of honey," Hattie said.

"What *is* that taste?"

"Buckwheat."

"Who's the genius that makes it?"

Hattie picked up the jar, turned it around once, and read the label: "Czapalay, Moncton, N. B."

"Very very good."

Alden looked at the painting over the buffet. The sea in which, or on which, the tall ship rode was a green so dark and ugly it was nearly black. Dark clouds blotted out the sky. The harbour, hinted at by the sketchiest of lighthouses, was otherwise non-existent.

Hattie began clearing things from the table, with loud sea-clashes. Five or six times she came and went, finally disappearing, with the two glass pitchers, one with milk, the other with orange juice, into the kitchen. The couple from Quebec slipped from the room and went up the stairs to prepare for the journey ahead. They seemed to be of one accord, after last evening's *contretemps*. Alden went through a pair of sliding doors into the sun-filled living room. Meredith sat alone at the table, in the window, eating her toast, drinking her coffee, and musing on the day ahead. She didn't seem to want to talk.

Susan was late delivering Gabriele. Alden kicked a beach ball back and forth in the front yard while he waited. The bells of the church on the side of the hill across the river rang out, in a spacious way that did nothing to break the sense of peace and quiet. Above the apple trees on the other side of the road Alden could see the little town with its accumulation of stores and services near the bridge. Nothing was moving. No one. Outside the church it was the same. Nothing doing. The sound of the bells was like music from a distant mountain, which only looks close because of perspective.

She drove a red Granada, with white sidewalls. She had overslept, she explained through the car window, without apology. She looked at Gabriele and when Gabriele did not move, she said, "You can get out now."

She circled the driveway and came back down to where Alden stood waiting with Gabriele. "I'll be back around five," she said to Alden. "Save a little room for supper," she said to Gabriele. They watched the Granada as it disappeared behind the old school building, re-emerged, crossed the bridge, turned right onto the road into Digby, and picked up speed. They listened to the sound of the car after the sight of it was lost behind the hill above the bend in the river. In the silence the sound, or the echo of the sound, could be heard for many miles, like an airplane overhead that has long since vanished from sight.

Alden carried two stones, each the size of his fist, up from the road, into the yard by the side of the house, to make a goal. He set them in the grass about two body lengths apart and, positioning himself as the goalkeeper, invited Gabriele to kick the ball at him "as hard as you can." The first few tries she was too slow, too hesitant, not sure which way to aim, but he kept after her, telling her to "give it a good kick," until she began to put something into it. "Kick it right on past me. Through me."

The first ones he blocked, then he let some by. One or two got by anyhow. "I'm not a hard man," he said to her. "But you've got to make an effort, otherwise I can't do anything for you." Then it was her turn to play in goal. "I can't do it," she said. But he insisted, and so, with a frown, she took up her post.

For half an hour they kicked the ball back and forth. Gabriele said nothing but played ferociously. Alden's few words might as well have been addressed to the goal post. Hattie called them inside to have lunch. She made sandwiches for them in the kitchen. The cat watched from the sill of an open window, ready to make his move – whether in or out – as quickly as need be. Hattie asked if they had any plans for after lunch.

Alden hadn't really thought about it. They might drive out to the beach. They might stop in Digby and look at the fishing boats.

"What does Gabriele want to do?"

"I don't know." He looked at Gabriele. "Gabriele, what do you want to do?"

She shrugged her shoulders. "I don't care."

"How old are you Gabriele," Hattie asked.

"Seven," she answered.

"I've got an idea," Alden said. "Let's drive out and say hello to your friend Stephen."

"Why?"

"I thought you might like to. I sure would."

"I don't care."

"It's your decision."

Gabriele looked at Hattie as if Hattie, in her wisdom, should have the answer. But Hattie only returned her look, frowning and pinching her mouth. "Child, it's up to you."

She sat there at the table, as mute as polished agate. She looked at the cat in the window. The cat purred loudly. "Okay," Gabriele said. Alden did not know if she was addressing him or the cat. Her task accomplished, her answer given, Gabriele pulled the chair up to the table and began to eat.

If only Hattie were always around, to show me the way. How easy everything would be.

Howard and Edna

*H*e climbed the hill out of town, following the road that ran towards Clementsport. He watched, as he'd been told, for the first turn-off on the right, and he came upon it suddenly, at the bottom of a short, sharp drop. A hundred yards up the dirt road, on the right, was the Lockerby house. Clinton's. It was a small white house, set back from the road, at the edge of a woods. In front, along one side of the driveway, was a row of white birch trees, like unburned candles. He got out of the car and walked towards the house.

Clinton's van was parked where he left it, by the side of the house. The house was shut tight, and there was a notice posted on the front door. *Crime Scene Stay Out.* The windows had new-looking aluminum storms. In the attic, at the top of the pitched roof, an aluminum ventilation plate reflected the sun.

A boy on a bicycle came towards them from the top of the dirt road. In the open door of the car Alden watched the rider as he came closer, in a cloud of dust. In the city people came and went, by car, by bus, by bicycle, on foot, and seldom did you pay any attention. Here in the country, along a lonely dirt road, one person, a child, alone in the distance, commanded an entire stage. The boundaries of any action were so much easier to make out.

The boy rode slowly down to where Alden was waiting. He stopped his bike at the edge of the road, where the driveway began. Alden closed the door of the car and came out to meet him. He told him his name.

The boy smiled at him as if he had been expecting him for a very long time. "I seen you at the funeral."

"I've brought someone with me."

The boy looked into the window of the car and when he saw Gabriele he smiled again, but it was a different kind of smile – bigger, gap-toothed, joyful. To Stephen if to no one else Gabriele was still Gabriele, no matter what trials might have befallen her. She was the same Gabriele who had always been his best friend.

"Look, why don't you and Gabriele play awhile, while I go up and talk to your Mom and Dad? How would that be?"

"They said they wouldn't be back till lunchtime."

"Maybe I'll get lucky."

Alden knocked on the window and Gabriele got out and came around. Stephen held his bike for her. "You want a ride?"

She got on the bike and pushed off, down the road towards the highway, and in a few seconds she had disappeared in a cloud of dust.

"Is that safe?"

"She's a good rider," Stephen assured him. "I should know."

"You, better than anyone," Alden said.

With a loud Ha! Stephen ran off after her.

*T*he back of the house faced the road. Alden knocked at the door but there was no answer. When he tried it, the door was open, so he went in. He found himself in a utility room. Against one wall, below a window, was a washing machine. Across from this, on a plank shelf, were a box of Tide, a bottle of Javex bleach, a can of copper polish, and a pair of garden clippers. In a corner stood a broom and a mop. "Watch your head when you come in," a voice called from the kitchen.

He entered a room so low his head grazed the ceiling. Edna wore a loose, faded-yellow, knee-length dress, and her hair was wrapped in yellow too, with a sort of bandana. She stood at the sink peeling potatoes, hard at work, her back to the door. She let the peel fall into the sink, the potatoes she dropped into a Dutch oven on the counter next to the sink. She was mostly lumps – or the suggestion of lumps – shoulders, mostly, and arms and buttocks. She did not turn around to look at him.

Across from the sink was an old-fashioned stove, converted to wood and oil, with a shiny, steel-grey flue feeding into the wall behind. At the other end of the room was a table, below a window, and by the table, to the right, a rocking chair. Behind the rocking chair a second doorway opened into the livingroom.

She fitted the top on the Dutch oven. As if just remembering that there was someone else in the room she said, "There's tea, you know, if you'd like."

He said he would.

She wiped her mud-brown hands on a cloth. From the rack of drying dishes behind the Dutch oven she took an earthenware mug for Alden to use. "Teapot's on the table."

He sat down at the table by the window. Edna came with a glass measuring cup, heavy with cream from the fridge. Lifting the cosy from the teapot, she felt to see if it was still hot, and poured him a cup.

The window looked out onto a bare field, which separated Howard and Edna from their neighbour. A vegetable garden took up a corner of the field near the house. The first green things – chives, sage, transplanted lettuce – were beginning to grow, and towards the back a line of stakes showed where pole beans would rise later and take hold.

"There's cookies, if you' d like." She set a plate of butter cookies on the table in front of him.

"Yum."

"Finish up that tea. Me and Howard's had all we want." The cream was a lumpy yellow, but cold and fresh and very good. It tasted much better than it looked.

"Them's homemade," Edna said, pushing the plate closer.

"Lovely," he mumbled, taking another.

From the living room (through the doorway behind the rocking chair) came the sound of a man coughing. Edna went back to the sink and resumed peeling potatoes, as if stung. Again the man coughed, but more loudly.

Alden looked through the open doorway into the living room. Howard came forward to the end of a couch, stopped a moment, coughed again, frowned, and tugged at the belt of his trousers. He came further forward, stepped into the doorway, and looked at Alden at the table and Edna at the sink. He was red-eyed from his nap. Alden started to get up.

"Stay sittin' ," he growled. "I'm not the bloody Queen, you know." With a dry, heavily lined face he came across and shook hands, almost driving Alden back into his chair.

"I seen you at the funeral." He was a thin, narrow-shouldered man, with a powerful grip. He had huge, heavily veined hands that were twice as big as Alden's.

"Gabriele stayed with us a few months, as you probably know."

"Awful mess. Awful."

"Howard, let the man drink his tea," Edna called from the sink, sharply.

"I ain't stoppin' him from drinkin' his tea." He tugged at his trousers again, as if worried they' d fall down. He sat in the rocking chair, took the pipe from the ashtray, and began filling it with tobacco. He had a funny way of working his hands, Alden thought, until he saw that the middle finger was missing, leaving a dark-brown, rounded stump about the size of a dime.

"It ain't much you can say about a man like that." He sat forward in the chair, his face as craggy, rocky, and vulnerable as the scrub pasture down the back of the house, behind the barn. His hair was cut close all around, except on top, where it was messed, and in front, where it was shaped into two broad, smooth waves, one piled on top of the other, brushed to the side.

"The papers suggest it was suicide."

Howard made fish-like, smacking sounds with his lips, as he lit his pipe. "I don't believe it for one second."

"You ..."

"The man didn't have the bloody guts to shoot himself."

"I undertand that Gabriele was the first one to find him."

"That was the worst thing of all."

"Did you hear the shot?"

"I did not hear the shot. I'll tell you the same thing I told them police: I did not hear the shot."

"What was he like?"

"Clinton? Well, I guess you could say he was kind of a mixed bag. Like they say, when he was good, he wasn't too bad, but when he was bad, he was somethin' awful."

"How did he and Gabriele get along?"

"I guess you heard them stories about how he mistreated her. Well, I guess he did. But I also know this for a fact: he tried. With the first two he had himself some real trouble, so I think he wanted to do it different with Gabby because Gabby was his last chance. It didn't work out too good, in the end."

"What kind of trouble?"

"They was always doin' things, gettin' into trouble. Specially that boy. Stealin' , skippin' school, drinkin' . Then he' d beat them. Still, it didn't seem to do no good."

"It was known that he beat his kids? Even then?"

"It weren't no secret. He didn't mind tellin' you hisself. He was just doin' what was right, to his way of thinkin' ."

"Right?"

"It's writ in the Bible, he claimed, that you got to lift up the rod against those you love."

"In the Bible?"

"That's what Clinton said. Beats me. I never could find it."

"You can read anything into the Bible."

"I reckon that to be a true statement."

"And he believed it?"

"He put it nicely to me once, when we was talkin' . He said, ' If they cross me I'll nail ' em.' I thought to myself, them's a fine choice of words, for a so-called Christian man. *Nail ' em.* And he meant it. Oh yes. He was a tough one, he was, or liked to pretend he was. When he was a boy, he said, he used to get up at four to milk the cows and walk to school, then after school there was more chores to do. ' It ain't never dawned on me to argue about chores,' he said, and I can remember the way he touched his forehead when he said them words, with three fingers, all bunched in a knot. A real hard tap, like to knock him out. ' Kids are spoiled nowadays,' he said. Well, we always think kids are spoiled nowadays, but if you ask me, it ain't true. Things change, that's all. Kids have different problems, and we don't even see them as problems, ' cause they ain't ours."

"Tell him about the girl," Edna said. She had done peeling potatoes but remained at the sink, with her back to it.

"That was the one time I really let him have it. That poor child. She wasn't but eight or nine when she came down with this sickness – scolio something. Some fancy name. The spine begins to curve in on itself and you can't do nothin' about it. Well, Clinton wouldn't let her see no doctor. Said whatever it was, he didn't care, it was the willa God. ' Ain't no way to solve these problems except Jesus,' was his way of puttin' it. He'd pray for her, that's what he'd do. Well, he musta prayed real hard, 'cause it didn't do a damn bita good. Then he found out about this vet over in Middleton, supposed to be some kinda faith healer. By Gawd, I bet that was some scene, with all them dogs barkin' out back, while he's in there tryin' to chase the devil out from this poor little girl, in the name of Jesus. Well, Clara, she was brought up Catholic, so she didn't go in for this brand of faith healin'. I guess that was some fight they had, right missus? I mean, Jesus H., you could hear 'em all the way over here. Well, she took that girl finally and they went to see a real doctor and they got her fixed up with some kinda brace and all. I told him, I did, to knock off the Jesus stuff before that girl was crippled for life. Well, I guess he seen the light. She's healed now and walks around like anybody. If she wasn't so huge."

"So what happened then? I mean, after the girl got the brace."

"Well, like I said, I guess he saw the handwritin' on the wall. He kinda laid off. Laid off the girl, that is. The boy, Christopher, well, that was a different story. They was always fightin'. So, one day, he just up and took off. Wasn't no more than sixteen. Couldn't stand it no more I guess. Spent a couple years in Ontario, I heard it said. Then he started showin' up around here again. Took up with one of them wimmin that lives over at that place they calls The Farm."

"What about Clinton? What happened to him?"

"Well, you know, it's a small town. Everybody knew all along what a bastard he was. I mean, beatin' up on kids, that's somethin' we don't do around here. No sir. So, after a while, he didn't have no more work. People didn't want him no more. Clara was still teachin' , so they weren't starvin' or nothin' . For the life of me I don't know why that woman stuck with him, mean bastard that he was. Maybe ' cause of that Catholic religion of hers, or some damn fool thing like that."

"So what did he do for work?"

"Oh, odd jobs."

"What kind of odd jobs?"

"Anything that came along. He did a fair amount of work for them wimmin that I was talkin' about, at The Farm. I guess odd is the right word, alright, if we're talkin' about them wimmin. Yes sir. They was hardworkin' though, I gotta give ' em that. They brought that place back from nothin' , they did. Clinton was over there quite a lot. They worked his balls off, that's what they did. And them two kids, they used to tease him somethin' awful, ' cause he was so shy. If them wimmin was queer, them two kids was downright mean. I know for a fact that that boy they got over there killed George Penner's cow."

"Oh posh," Edna said. "You don't know no such thing."

"I do. I seen the bullet that George dug outta that animal. There ain't no other rifle like the one that boy has got. I'll tell yuh this much, ever since they went and give him that rifle, I ain't felt safe around here."

"Why not have a word with the mother?"

Howard laughed. "I guess Gabby didn't tell you diddly-squat. Me tell that woman her son ain't up to no good? She' d have my balls."

Edna coughed.

"Excuse my French," Howard said.

"You talk about two kids. Did you see any sign of the father."

"They ditched the father back in the States. Like I said, they was queer."

He emptied his pipe into the glass ashtray. "Oh, they's done some things," he said, dramatically. "Yes sir, they's done some things."

"What kind of things?"

"Bad things."

"Such as?"

"There was this piece of land across the road that George wanted to buy, so's he could graze his sheep. Damned if them wimmin didn't find out about it and put in an offer of their own. More' n George could afford, by far."

"That land was right next door to them," Edna said. "They don't want no sheep grazin' in their backyard."

"Backyard! Hell, that land of theirs is all overgrown back in there. They don't make no use of it whatsoever."

"Sure, and it was a couple sheep of yours that poor George was gonna git stuck with."

"Weren't no profit in it for me, you know that."

"Still, it don't mean nothin' ."

"Well, then there was that rotary tiller that belonged to Morris. He lent them that till in good faith, and they just keep it and keep it, never give it back, when they know he's waitin' for it, and when he comes to get it, it's broke. And they don't make no apology. They pretend nothin's wrong. And Morris, well, he's a quiet man, he ain't one for makin' much of a fuss, that's the way he is, so he just takes it and don't say nothin'. They never offered to get it fixed or nothin'. Me, I would've took my gun along and conducted some business."

"They's lookin' out for themselves," Edna said. "Like we all do."

"Sure, they's lookin' out for themselves, but not the way we all do. No mam. That's where your mistake is. Tell me this, if they's just lookin' out for themselves the way we all do, where they git all that money they got? You seen that brandnew pick-up truck. And that brick shithouse of a freezer in the basement. All that expensive electronical equipment. Where they git the money for all that stuff? Nobody else got that kinda money. It sure as hell ain't comin' from that farm of theirs. They don't make one red penny the way they run that farm."

"Maybe they had that money when they come up here. Maybe they got somebody down there in them States that sends ' em money. Maybe they git somma that alimony."

"I'll tell you what it is, if you really want to know." He put a match to his cold pipe. "Drugs, that's what it is. They's into drugs. That's where they git all their money. Drugs."

"Oh, go on."

"Tell me this then, if you're so smart. Why all those hippies hangin' out over there? Plain trash, the lot of them, if you ask me."

"Nobody's askin' you."

"They over there for the fresh air, or what? Plenty of fresh air where they come from."

"That don't prove nothin' ."

"Course it don't prove nothin' . I ain't tryin' to prove nothin' . This ain't no court of law, is it? I'm just tellin' you what I know."

"What you think you know."

"What I know."

Edna turned away from her husband, opened the lid to the Dutch oven, checked the potatoes for progress, put the lid back on, and turned down the heat. She stood with her arms folded under her heavy breasts, signalling she was done talking. She' d already said too much. Let Howard do the talking. She only provoked him and he didn't like that.

"How sure are you about this?" Alden asked.

"Just as sure as I'm sittin' here and you're sittin' there."

"What kind of drugs?"

"Pot. Hash. Coke. You name it. They're big time, that's what I'm tellin' you."

"What about Christopher? How does he fit into it?"

"The way I got it figured he's the one doin' the transportin' . Half the time he's gone, ' looking for work' is what they tells me but I don't buy it. Quebec, Ontario. Back and forth, back and forth. Well, it ain't too hard to guess what he's up to."

"Maybe you should take it to the police."

"The police know. You bet they know. It ain't that easy to prove, that's the thing. They ain't stupid."

A truck drove up the driveway and stopped just under the kitchen window. Edna looked out. "It's Morris," she said.

Howard put his pipe face down in the ashtray, got up from the rocking chair, and went to the window, pushing Edna aside. "About time too," he said, gruffly. He went out the back door, which was at the front of the house, to greet his friend.

"He's come to git his mower looked after," Edna explained. "Needs sharpenin' about once a year. I guess they'll be chewin' the fat awhile."

"It's time for us to start back anyway."

Edna frowned. "Them kids is havin' such a good time."

"Susan said she'd be back at five to get Gabriele."

"It ain't that late, is it?"

"I thought I'd stop at The Farm on the way back. I'd like to see for myself."

Edna thought about this a moment but decided not to say anything. "Suit yourself."

"I'll see what Gabriele wants to do." He looked through the door into the living room. "Can I get out this way?"

"Last time I looked."

"Thanks for the cup of tea."

"You come and see us again, hear?"

*T*he living room opened onto the field behind the house. A rutted driveway, still muddy from recent rain, led straight back to the shed. Beyond the field was woods. Morris, pushing his mower, went inside the shed. Howard went in after him and closed the door. Gabriele and

Stephen were playing in a tent near the garden, giggling and screeching.

Alden walked down the driveway to the road and started along the road. Two hundred yards from Howard and Edna's was a T-intersection, and he turned and walked towards The Farm. As he approached he could see a red barn, a grey, weathered house with a steep roof opposite the barn, and a shed behind the house, in corrugated aluminum. Along one side of the house were three tall, well-shaped cypress trees. Behind the barn was a set of chicken coops. Behind the chicken coops was a vegetable garden. A pick-up truck was parked in the driveway in front of the barn. A swing was attached to an oak tree in the front yard. There did not seem to be anyone around.

He went a little way along that road and stopped. *What am I doing here? What am I looking for? What do I care about any of these people, Christopher included? What does any of this have to do with me?*

Just then someone came out and got into the truck. He dropped down into a ditch by the side of the road. *Admit it. You're damned scared.*

From the ditch he watched as the truck lurched back, turned onto the road, and started away, towards the town. A cloud of dust swallowed it.

He climbed out of the ditch and went back the way he had come. The legs of his pants were covered with dozens of purple-flowering, globular, tenacious thistle heads.

Sheriff

"*M*y father gave me a choice," Meredith, at the breakfast table, was talking, for the benefit of those assembled, including Hattie, Alden, and a new guest, a retired man from Sidney, Cape Breton Island, Alan, who had arrived Sunday evening with plans to spend a few days in Elk River where he had friends before going on to Yarmouth and from Yarmouth by ferry to Bar Harbour, then inland several hundred miles to a wilderness lake where he had rented a cabin for a week and where he expected his son, who was working in the States, in Chesapeake Bay, as a fisherman or fisherman's apprentice, to join him, talking of herself, a subject she found endlessly fascinating. "Take the subway or use the family limousine. His only condition was that if I should choose the limousine, I was to be let out not a block away from school, or two blocks away, but right at the front door, where all the other kids went in. He made his point and I've never forgot it: there's nothing to be ashamed of just because you're rich. Hold your head up high and do what's right.

"My father was a businessman. I respected him but had no intention of following in his footsteps. I was fed up with always being thought of as 'macDougall's kid.' I chose journalism as a profession because I was a sucker for the printed word. I couldn't wait to get out on my own. I wanted the best education so I chose Columbia. The school didn't live up to its reputation, but the city, what a shocker that was. It was like suddenly everything was alive for the first time. This was the real world at last. I mean, here I was, a kid from Toronto, but it was like this was the first time I had ever really opened my eyes. In Toronto it's like it's so much harder to see what's going on, to *feel* what's going on. In New York everything seemed possible, everything was up for grabs. Among millions, the individual mattered.

"When I got back to Toronto, I was determined to do something that would make a difference. I could rule out political reporting. Ditto, the ' world of women.' Regional disparity seemed a topic worthy of my attention, in every sense of the word. Pockets of poverty in a land of plenty was a juicy scandal. My first assignment took me to the Gaspé Peninsula. I've also spent some time on the Island, and with the Plains Indians. This is my first visit to Nova Scotia.

"Let me tell you about a woman I got to know in Glace Bay. Her name was Ida. Ida MacKenzie. Maybe you know her." She looked at Alan, but Alan shook his head.

"She wasn't yet fifty, but she looked seventy. Physically she was a wreck. Poor eating habits, brute of a husband, the works. Diabetic. Obese. I mean, big. We had some very interesting talks. Just before I was to leave she had a stroke, which left her paralyzed on one side. She couldn't talk. I sat with her for three days, and the whole time she just stared at me, unable to utter a word. That really shook me, I must say.

"The most exciting thing I've discovered in the last six years since I began writing is that I have a talent for the job. I may be loaded but I can also make my own way. My father says I write like an angel."

No one said a word when Meredith finished speaking. Hattie held the cat, Lord Randall, in her lap, and it was hard to tell which of the two might have been less interested in Meredith's story, the woman or the cat. Alan sat back in his chair, his head tucked down, his arms folded on his chest, his eyes closed, as if dreaming. Alden finished his breakfast without appetite. Everything tasted dry, like straw.

Meredith bothered him. All the way into Annapolis Royal (he was going into town to see the sheriff, and afterwards, he hoped, spend some time with Gabriele) he tried to think what it was about Meredith that angered him so. She called herself a writer and maybe she was. She seemed serious. Apparently she was productive. She was arrogant, yes, but there was something else. It was her idea of writing. Writing to her was a job like any other job. Maybe in a sense it was a job but the kind of writing he was trying to do was different. It wasn't a job, it was a way of discovering hidden corners of the world and of himself. Maybe she was looking for hidden corners, but not the ones inside where it mattered. They were all out there, in the world. She made it sound so easy, so routine. "I write like an angel!" What bullshit!

No wonder she could talk and talk, always about herself. And no wonder, when he gave himself up to her idea of writing (as he was tempted to do), he could write and write and never feel that he was getting anywhere, never feel that he was able to make things come alive. He was scratching the surface, leaving little claw marks – nothing more. Writing has to get below the surface, below the clichés and the half-baked conclusions. Her whole purpose in life seemed to be to obscure this truth.

No one knew where the sheriff was. The receptionist buzzed his office but got no answer. The deputy, Roy, said he believed he' d gone home. He hadn't seen him since early morning, when they' d had a cup of coffee together. It would be best to come back another day. He went outside again and not knowing what else to do, walked around the block and came back around to the back of the building.

A set of black metal steps led down to the asphalt parking lot. A police car, white with green trim, was parked near the back door, at a forty-five degree angle to the building. A second police car, this one all black with chrome trim, sat at the back of the lot, in a corner under a tree, with its hood up. It was a four-door Plymouth Valiant. A large, barrel-chested man, dressed in jeans and a white crew-neck T-shirt, was bent down over a fender working the engine.

All six spark-plug wires hung loose. The man removed each plug in turn, cleaned it, and re-set the gap. He put each plug back in place, tightened it with a socket wrench, and pushed the wire cap down over the tip of the plug. He came around (still not looking at Alden on the other side), got in the car, and tried the motor. It would not start.

The sign on the back of the building next to the police station said "Morse Teas" in red letters on a white background. A figure stood in the window on the second floor, looking out. Inside the car the man leaned forward, his barrel chest pushing hard up against the steering wheel, his hand and arm down and under (as if under a woman's skirt: the expression on his face that hard, that focused) as he turned the ignition, grinding the motor, for ten seconds, fifteen seconds, twenty. It would not start.

"Son-of-a-bitch," his lips said. He got out and came around to the front of the car, where he stopped and stared at Alden as if aware of him for the first time. His tiny green eyes did a disappearing act under ridged brows. He let the hood fall with a bang. He said nothing. He walked past him, across the parking lot, and in through the door at the back of the station.

Shaken, Alden stood there a moment before following him to the door and stepping inside the station for a second time. Roy, the deputy he'd met, a small, pale-skinned man with thin hair and thin, delicate fingers, was pinning a notice to the dark-brown, cork bulletin board in the hallway. "I don't know what happened out there," he said, "but if I was you I'd come back another day."

"I don't have another day," Alden said.

Roy showed him to a small, bare room. "Wait here," he said.

In the middle of the room was a card table, with a red-and-white checked oilcloth as a cover. Four mismatched metal chairs surrounded the table. A window, hung with a ruffled, red-and-white checked curtain, looked out to the parking lot. Alden pulled one of the chairs out, sat down, and waited.

The sheriff wore dark trousers and a dark shirt with a badge pinned to the bottom of the shirt pocket. He sat with his back to the window. "You got somethin' to say, say it." He drummed his fingers on the checked oilcloth.

Hot, dizzy, he wanted to get up and leave but something tied him to the small, tight mouth, the high, prominent cheekbones, the hard, green eyes that mocked him, the massive cranium with its black hair cut close like the fur of a rabbit. It was almost a mumble when he finally said, "I heard some things."

"Things?"

"Maybe Clinton didn't shoot himself."

He sat back with a mischievous grin on his face. "All I been hearin' this whole fuckin' week is Clinton Lockerby, Clinton Lockerby. Tell me somethin' new."

"I don't know if what I have to say is new or not."

"Go on."

"What I hear is that some neighbours of Clinton's are involved."

"Are they now?"

"There's a place up the road they call The Farm. Seems it could be a cover for some drug dealers from the States."

"Been hearing the same shit for years. You don't want to know how many times we been out there, checkin' it out."

"But this time there's been a death. Maybe that might mean something."

The sheriff made a noise that seemed to come up from deep in his chest, as if he might choke or vomit. He turned his head a little to one side and snarled, "I guess we don't need you comin' round and tellin' us how to do our job."

"I'm not telling you how to do your job. I'm telling you what I hear."

"Who are you?"

"Clinton's little girl stayed with us before Clinton grabbed her back. I want her back."

"I wouldn't go meddlin' if I was you."

"I think I should talk to someone else. You don't seem very interested."

"You do that. And good luck to you." He got up and went out of the room.

Waves

A city park lay halfway up the steep hill, and above the park, a church. At the bottom of the hill a river ran swirling mud-brown towards a low, flat, iron bridge. He climbed the hill in search of something – his car. His breathing came in short, shallow gasps. His heart thumped irregularly. He could feel it. Thump, thump, pause, thump.

He turned a corner and went on to the next, mechanically. He was not conscious of his destination. He had no conscious destination. At the edge of town he crossed a foot bridge and below the foot bridge the same dark river flowed by: this was not the way. He turned and went back.

He walked, circling back, retracing his steps, venturing where traffic was busiest, until he came to the black and white gate of Fort Anne National Park. Somehow this seemed right, so he went in. He remembered: he was going to meet Susan and Gabriele at the fort, and the three of them would have lunch together. Then Gabriele and he would spend the afternoon at the beach. Susan had some errands to do. She'd wait for them at a restaurant near the fort, where she wanted to take Gabriele for supper. It all came flooding back: the discussion with Susan, yesterday, in the window of the car. He took a deep breath, opened his eyes, and looked around him. *But where did I park my car? I can't remember. What's wrong with me?*

He was supposed to meet them at eleven, but it was already a quarter after. He went inside the museum but changed his mind and came back outside. He went along a path by the river, towards the back of the park. It was all hills and grass. On top of the biggest hill there were several twenty-millimeter cannons, looking out over the river. He climbed halfway up the hill and sat there with his arms around his knees and waited.

*R*oy, still in uniform (dark trousers and dark shirt), strolled along Water Street, at the bottom of the hill below the police station. In front of a Chinese restaurant he stopped and talked with a passerby. In the window of the Simpson's Catalogue Centre he paused to look at the display of washing machines. He held the door of the Bank of Montreal for a woman with a baby in a stroller. At the end of the block he circled an empty telephone booth. He looked back the way he had come. When he saw that the sidewalk was deserted, he stepped inside the booth and closed the door.

He fumbled in his pocket until he found a dime. He put the dime in the slot and dialed a number. He took a wad of chewing tobacco from a pouch in his shirt pocket and stuffed it into one side of his mouth. The voice that answered was soft, muffled, indefinite. "Yes?" it said.

"Who's speaking," Roy said.

"Janice."

"It's me."

Janice clicked her tongue in annoyance. "You were told not to call this number."

"It's important."

"Well, what is it?"

"Some creep was in here talkin' to the sheriff. Said didn't we know about you people out there."

"Know what?"

"Said you was probably the ones that went and shot old Clinton."

"Who was this *creep*?"

"Said his name was Alden something. Sounded like *auld lang syne*."

"Alden what? Use your brain for a moment and think."

"Oakes."

"He was at the funeral."

"Better arrange another one."

"Cool it. Nothing has changed."

"Okay, you're the boss. But don't forget: I told you."

"I won't forget. And don't call here again, do you understand?"

"Like I say, you're the boss."

*T*he waves were too high for Gabriele. She played at the edge, getting her feet wet, but refused to go farther out. Alden lifted her onto his back and carried her out. She clung to his neck, choking him. The floor gave way to deeper water but so gradually they almost didn't notice it. The waves splashed her feet and her legs. When she felt the cold hit her legs she screeched. Sinking to his knees he lowered her by degrees into the water but she would not let go. He dived forward into the cold water. She would not let go. She felt safe because she had hold of him. "Do it again," she said. She was excited because she had done what she didn't think she could do. He dived in again, though not deep, and she went with him. She buried her face in his back.

After a time he brought her out and left her by the edge of the water to play. He sat on a blanket at the top of the beach, blue and shaking with cold. He wrapped his towel around his shoulders. With a stick she dug a hole in the wet sand. He could still feel her hands around his neck, the fingers like claws, never letting go. He sat hunched forward, holding his knees. The sun was warm on his back, then it was hot.

It was Monday, and the beach was not crowded. Already it was hard to believe that he had met someone like the sheriff who had tried to grind him into dust. *I know nothing about how people live and think in this part of the province. It's like another country.*

If he could not talk to the sheriff, who could he talk to? *In an hour I'll forget what happened and remember only this moment, this beach, this hot sand. Gabriele at play. Or I'll remember what happened, only to tell myself that it never happened and will never happen again.*

He watched the waves spill onto the beach behind Gabriele. He was hungry but did nothing about it. Instead of listening to the cravings of his body he decided to listen to the sounds all around him, the ones he never used to listen to, he was so busy. The water sweeping in, crashing onto the sand, sinking into silence, washing back out again as with an intake of breath through gritted teeth. The gulls calling out, almost a shriek, wheeling and turning high over the water, or sweeping low. A dog barking, far down the beach, a thin, flat bark that matched, with a delay of a second or two, the upward snap of its head. A man laughing with his eight-year-old boy, as they batted a ball back and forth over a net. The buzz of flies. The wind. The pulse of blood in the bone behind his ear.

It occurred to him that he might die, he or his body, it was the same thing, that he might die, sitting there on the beach, in the hot sun. And somehow, in some way that reason could not prove to him, this had to do with whether or not he kept his eyes open. He felt he must do everything in his power to keep his eyes open. Yet all the forces around him, the sun, the sea, the sounds he was hearing for the first time, invited him to close his eyes and sleep. He feared this sleep, from which he might never wake.

There was something in him that was soggy and fibrous, and to close his eyes, to doze, would be to give himself up to this part of himself. But he also felt that in him was something tougher than this, something rope-like, stronger than he had ever given himself credit for, but that it was much harder to hold on to this part of himself, but that if he did not, he would die.

The sun was low in the sky. It had arrived there in the flicker of an eyelid. He had no recollection of the hours that must have passed. He stood up and looked around. The beach was nearly empty. Gabriele played at the water's edge. She ran out, caught an armful of water, splashed herself, then ran back in, shrieking. Her long hair, in braids, was wet through and through. She enjoyed taking one of these braids and squeezing it until the water came out. He called to her to come up and when she did, he dried her with a towel and gave her a sip of water from the jug.

Hattie

*S*usan waited in front of the restaurant across the street from the fort. Kneeling, Alden hugged Gabriele. "If you want to come back with me ... We could leave anytime you want ... In the morning ..."

She squinted at him, fighting the bright sun that was reflected in the window of the restaurant. "In the morning?"

"In the morning, in the afternoon, the day after tomorrow. It's up to you."

She thought a moment, then said: "Can I think about it?"

"There's no rush." He looked at Susan. "I'm not going anywhere."

"Maybe tomorrow."

"Sure, tomorrow. Or the next day."

Susan and Gabriele went into the restaurant. Alden drove away, up the hill, out of town. The more distance he put between himself and the girl, the closer he felt to her. She was afraid, for good reason. She was like a small woodlands animal, set, at any moment, to take flight. Leap from the limb of a tree to the ground below if necessary. But what about him? What was he afraid of? How could she trust him if he could not trust himself?

He hung his towel on the clothesline to dry and went up the stairs to his room. On the table by the window, against the glass of violets, was a note, in Hattie's hand. *Janice called. You're invited for supper tomorrow at The Farm. They said bring Gabby.*

He knew he would go, but he was a little afraid. Still, he wanted to go, to see for himself what it was like, what *they* were like. To find out if what Howard had said was true.

He put on fresh clothes and went downstairs. The cat, Lord Randall, was curled up on a step in the warm sun. He opened one eye to look at him, and closed it. From the living room came the sound of someone playing the piano. When he went in, he found Hattie sitting on the couch, knitting. A vase of wildflowers, a portable radio, and a scattering of magazines covered the larger part of the glass coffee table. A large, brown paper bag set on the floor under the table contained her knitting materials.

Her hands were so small they could be put into small-mouth jars. As she knitted, these hands moved with a quick up-and-down, wave-like motion, with a little twist of the wrist at the top of each wave, that was as precise and profluent as the ticking of a clock. The music on the radio and the movement of her own arm held her in a kind of trance, and he had the good sense not to say anything. He sat in the rocking chair and watched her knit. The music was Mozart – a piano concerto. What a happy, brilliant, glittering work it was! He was happy to sit and listen and not say a word.

But when the music came to an end and the news came on, without warning, without delay, it was a shock. It was much too loud. A fire in the mountains above Santa Barbara had burned many homes. A man in Portland, Oregon, had shot and killed three co-workers before killing himself. The value of the dollar had fallen for the third day in a row. "How very depressing," Hattie said, turning down the volume. "Can't they tell us something happy for a change?"

The sweater she was knitting was for a grandchild, a boy of five, who was coming for a visit. His name was Michael and he lived in Calgary with his father, Hattie's son, Ian. Because there was no work in rural Nova Scotia, Ian had taken his family to Alberta to find work. Things had gone from bad to worse, however, when Ian's wife had started seeing other men out there. One day she just disappeared. Now Ian had his hands full, with a job and a child to raise. "I feel lucky if he gets back once a year for a visit."

"You miss him a lot, I can tell."

"You remind me of him a little. He's not as tall as you and he doesn't have a beard, but you have the same blue eyes, that seem to say, yes, I want to know what you're thinking."

"Sometimes they're blue, sometimes they're green."

"There's something different about you too. When I look in your eyes, I see something hard, like glass. You have the idea that you need that, if you want to get anywhere in life. You remind me of my husband, Matthew, in that regard. Matthew was tall too, like you. And Matthew had hard eyes, and he knew when he had to be hard, to get what he wanted. Ian is more like me, rounder and softer – too soft if you ask my opinion. Matthew had to be hard because he was in real estate. In real estate you want to look soft and act hard, and Matthew was like that. When he was dying, when he knew he was dying, he did a hard thing for me, which I'll never forget. He bought this house for a song, because he knew I didn't want to be a burden to anyone.

With me he could be soft because he knew where he stood. I made it easy for him."

Hattie had one other child, a daughter, Cathy, with whom she had very little contact. Except for cards at Christmas, they did not exist for each other, though they lived fewer than fifty miles apart. Cathy had a husband and children and a house to look after. She was busy doing all the right things, and she didn't have time for Hattie. For Hattie was not "responsible," the way she sank everything into the bed and breakfast, which was a marginal business proposition at the best of times. More and more money down the drain, and for what? An old woman wanted to be "independent." The cost of such independence was too high, in Cathy's opinion.

Hattie could live with a lot. She could live with Cathy's greed. She could live with the fact that Cathy's husband (a certified horse doctor, a sometime preacher, and a self-proclaimed faith healer) was the biggest fraud in the valley. She could live with the fact that of Cathy's four children, not one of them was likeable. But what she could not live with was the fact that Cathy focused her animosity not on her (Hattie) but on Hattie's cat, whom she had correctly identified as Hattie's weak point.

Matthew's job meant that he was often away, late into the night, showing properties to clients. Hattie would get lonely and therefore she was glad when Lord Randall came into her life. A gift from a client of Matthew's, Lord Randall was a kitten when she got him, but he was already a Lord. She became instantly more sociable and happy, as the beast as she called him was always making friends with somebody down the block, or staying out all night, so that she had to go and look for him and knock on doors. She exchanged cat lore with cat lovers, and got to know her neighbours. He got into fights, so she spent half her time bandaging and nursing her poor Lord Randall. The cat was soon a veteran warrior, with a torn ear, patches of missing fur and in general a ragged look to him.

He was a white cat and his eyes were small and yellow. She fed him too much, or he found too much to eat on his nightly escapades, and he grew fat: a far cry from the darker, more shapely pedigree cats she saw going in and out of neighbours' houses. But he was independent, and often caught mice, or chickadees, or baby robins when they fell out of trees, and he didn't mind when she scolded him, and he purred and cuddled when she held him to her at those times she suffered loneliness.

Once she realized that her children had left her, that they had their own lives to live, and their own thoughts to think, and no longer needed, or even wanted her, she accepted it, and a bitterness that was always softened by self-derision welled up at times like Christmas. She sang to the cat, "You nasty old cat, you filthy old beast, no one wants you now do they Lordie, no, you're just an alley cat, just an old thieving cat. Hey Lordie! Lordie! Lordie!"

Now it was no joke. He was old, as old as she was in "cat years." Which meant it cost some when he got sick. Nephritis was a persistent problem, which could require surgery. All Cathy could see was more money being wasted, and for what? An ugly old fat cat that was going to die anyway, in a year or two. The cat was like the house

– a losing proposition. When she talked like that, Hattie's blood boiled. The bitch! How dare she!

She said the best thing would be to get someone to "put him out of his misery." Because he was old didn't give her the right to talk about him like that, like he was a sack of potatoes that you threw out when they went rotten, just because he cost something when he got sick. (It wasn't too hard to figure out who that "someone" might be, who would consent to "put him out of his misery." It was all the same to that man, as long as it paid.)

The motion of her hands ceased. Her eyes were blank, dead. Her jaw had dropped, and seemed out of proportion to the rest of her small face, as if she were preparing herself, mentally, for a fight, but a fight she would have to wage only in her sleep, unconsciously. The news on the radio came to an end: a voice read out the weather report, but it was one day out of date.

Alden sat forward in the chair. The chair squeaked, waking Hattie from her sleep. She looked at him, the bearded, green-eyed man. She smiled, he smiled back. She licked the corner of her mouth where she felt something wet, a trickle of saliva. Music played on the radio. Something from a piece called "Petroushka." She picked up her knitting.

"Did you get to the beach today?" she asked.

He told her the name of the beach: Sandy Cove.

"It's been a long time since I've been to the beach."

There was a noise in the hallway. Alan, the retired man from Sidney, on his way up the stairs to his room, had startled the cat, setting off a chain reaction of hisses and harsh words, each angrier than the last. His two hands up, his fingers curled in like claws, as if applying a hex, Alan, laughing, hissed back, "Whiskey spitter! Catch her, catch her, yellow-eyed scratcher!"

Hattie got up and went out, to see what it was. "Must be somebody's supper time," she said through the rails, apologizing. "He gets a mite touchy."

"Don't bother me none," Alan said, and when the cat hissed again, showing yellow teeth to go with yellow eyes, he sang: "Atter, atter, sleeky flatterer! Spitfire chatterer, scatter her, scatter her off her mat!" This was sufficient to silence Lord Randall, who skirted the enchanted man, bounced black-eyed down the stairs, and scooted along the hallway into the kitchen.

"See, now I've scared her away."

"He will do no destruction if he is well fed," Hattie said, and followed the beast into the kitchen. "Nor will he spit without provocation."

Alan continued up the stairs, singing: "Run till dithery! Hithery! Thithery!"

All twelve pounds of him, grown round and thick with desire, purred in the kitchen. The white saucer like a full moon descended from the clouds of the table above. Nestled over the shining rim, he buried his chin in the creamy sea. His tail hung loose: each drowsy paw was doubled under each bending knee. His world was a vast shapeless white, till his tongue had curled the last delicious drop.

Blasted Remnants

*T*he light glittered on the dry chips of leaves that bunched closely wherever the ground dipped down and away from the road. Bird calls sounded high above as if from the mid-morning's unstrung throat itself. Then they were at the brook. It had a braided surface, with a central strand of current cutting into the still water below the bridge and constantly pushing back the lather of the foam scum lapping there by the bank. All along the bank tufts of dead grass hung like nests in the bushes, marking the high-water level of last spring's floods. And then, beyond the brook, by the edge of the woods, there was the blessing-pink of the hawthorn blossoms.

Gabriele stretched her legs in the prickly grass. At her back the hedge grew tall and wild with flowers. At her feet a pond shaded rust-green between a pile of stones and the stump of a tree. By the edge of the road, where the pond drained, two budworm-dead, big-tooth aspens made a V above a leaning white-flaked tombstone. Across the bumpy, dog-dumb field the blasted remnants of the old farmhouse lay as if on a long-forgot battleground.

While Gabriele, safe in the tuft of grass below the hedge, ate her sandwich and her fries, Alden turned towards the edge of the woods, where the sound of the axe cutting into the trees grew louder. The edge fell so bluntly – chomp chomp chomp – on nerves the morning had set just right for memory that he stayed the blood-flow of thought a moment and listened. For a moment now he *was* that axe-wielding man deep in the woods, ages ago. It was here he' d sought asylum when the news was brought home to him that his father, half a world away in a Halifax hospital, was gone. It was here, below the clustering hawthorne, that he'd lifted his voice to cold heaven. It was here, beneath the aspen and the spruce, that he'd felt the centre slip, the light grow dim.

He came near to the dip in the path where the fence used to cross. He had thought he would remember its every up and down, but the years and the unchecked ferns and scrub maple had taken over. It was an unknown woods that faced him now. He bent and lifted the wires apart, passing between them. On the other side he straightened up, mimicking the red spruce. He felt possessed by something that his conscious mind had no part in. He saw Jason walking ahead of him on the path in his high yellow boots. He kept walking and walking and would not stop or look around. There was something defiant in the way he pushed on, without pause, without complaint, in the heavy boots. Straight, steady, too proud.

He hurried to catch up to him. They walked awhile together in the silent woods. A carpet of spruce needles cushioned their going. Below them lay the swamp, which they would soon have to cross. He said, "Do you want to rest a moment?" But the person who turned to him was not Jason but Lise, and he remembered the look on her face when on occasion he'd seen her teeth glisten with the thought, *What became of the way my second child would have looked, if she had been born alive?*

He wrenched his head sideways, as if dodging an arrow. Then she was crying and he put his hand to her shoulder but she shook free and ran ahead into the woods alone. A deer stood watching him on a hill above the path, brushed slick as a flower with alertness, held still as a stone with unknowing, it gazed at him, between slatted layers of trees. He saw in its eyes that trampling look of animals braving their distrust of people in the force of circumstance. He saw its hair, and that it was not silken but coarse. But there was something about this coarseness that made him glad: it was real. It was almost as if the creature, in its coarseness, were asking him to stay near, to come close. A bird, perched invisibly in the spruce above him, gave voice to the deer's dumb cry. The singing (two even notes, one high, one low, more like whistling than anything else) sounded so clear in the hollow of the woods that it was as if it came from within him not from without. Then it was not the bird singing that he heard but Gabriele calling him, in her small, faraway, timid voice, that was also like singing, but singing that she twisted, in her fear, into the shape of a question mark. When he looked again, the deer was gone.

"You shouldn't have left me," she said when he came back.

Her eyes were red-clouded with crying. He held her in the dust of the road (where she had climbed, looking for him) and he said, "I was there all the time."

"I didn't see you," she said.

How long has she been calling me?

The thought of her calling him and getting no answer stabbed him so deeply that he said, "Forgive me."

Then she was herself again, sniffing her tears away, wandering down into the field to pick up the sandwich wrappings and the paper bag she had left there beneath the hedge. But the fries, which she had not finished because of her fright when she couldn't see him or find him, she dumped out into the grass for the flock of birds, starlings, that flew out to her now, from the abandoned farmhouse.

The Farm

*A*my came out to meet them when they turned into the driveway. She took Gabriele by the hand and led her away into the barn – dragged her. Alden started up the steps of the porch but stopped when he saw the dog, a black Labrador retriever, its mouth open and pink tongue drooling. Janice, at the screen door, laughed. "He's friendly," she said, and the dog, as if to prove the point, lay down again, with its long, shiny-black nose snug to the floor, its eyes half open, half closed.

"Come on in, he won't bite." He followed her into the kitchen. She cut him a slice of lemon and a fresh mint leaf for his gin and tonic. The red pepper on the cutting board was cut in half and each half sliced into thin strips. He offered to help if there was more cutting or peeling to be done but she said, "Everything's under control." She scraped the red pepper into a bowl with the other cut vegetables.

He wandered into the next room on his own. A turntable sat on a pine chest under the window, side by side with a stereo tuner. Against the wall below the stairway was a bookcase full of books. He stood with tilted head, looking at titles, sipping his drink. "Nice collection of books you've got," he called into the kitchen.

"Yes," she called back. "The only thing we miss about city life is books and music."

On the table by the couch was a copy of a recent edition of *The Whole Earth Catalogue*, in black paper. He opened it at random. On page two hundred thirty-three was a picture, in different shades of grey, of a man and a woman alone in a very cluttered geodesic dome, which was made of strips of wood and sheets of clear plastic film. The woman was naked, and lay with her knees up, her feet tucked under, on a kind of bed, her belly swollen in advanced pregnancy. The man sat in a chair, both feet resting on a mound of solid-caked mud. He was shirtless, with long hair and, in profile, a hooked nose. On the dirt floor beneath the bed were (among other, lesser items) a white plastic container of the kind used to pour windshield wiper fluid, a live rooster, and a very big cast-iron pot with a lid. The picture was entitled "Aquarian Haven." The text above the picture described something called "The Outlaw Area."

Bernice, Amy's mother's friend, came down the stairs so softly that she startled him. "The editor is an old friend of ours," she said, seeing the catalogue open on the table. "This was many years ago, when we lived in Boston."

He turned the page. In the middle column, at the top of the page, was a review of a book entitled *The Drug Bust*. "Why did you leave?"

She came closer, seeming intent on shutting the book. Her face, with its large, brown eyes, prominent cheekbones, and strong chin, seemed all bones and hollows between bones. She had the size and heft to suggest she could be the mother of Amy, not Janice. "When we moved to Boston things were beginning to happen. But the difference was, we weren't just watching things happen, we were making them happen. But as more and more elements came into it, things got more and more insane. On the one hand we were doing some extremely useful work in this place we called the BAWC, standing for Boston

Area Women's Collective. But we lived in this kind of tight, insular way where we always felt we had to defend ourselves from physical and other sorts of abuse. There didn't seem to be any way out of it. Also, we were into a lot of drugs. You almost had to be at that time. It became very very difficult. We didn't feel like going back to Michigan, or wherever it was we came from, so we thought we' d come here."

"Why here? Why Nova Scotia?"

"We had nothing more to pin our hopes on than those three beautiful cypress trees by the side of the house, which said in a loud, clear voice that someone had lived here before and prospered. We were still a little afraid of being disappointed as we circled the house. We found a vegetable garden where nothing grew except cow vetch and daisies. The old wagon shed had fallen down but the big wood-and-aluminum barn was still standing, and against it an empty chicken-run with streamers of orange plastic caught in the netting-wire. Remnants of garbage bags.

"Front and back doors were locked. One of us put an elbow through a windowpane, loosened the latch, and stepped inside. We wandered from room to room. Except for some large pieces of furniture – dressers, wardrobes, beds – there was nothing. Our feet left prints on the floor. When we entered the kitchen there was a flurry of wings as birds flew out a hole in the roof. Droppings lay everywhere. The floor grumbled when we walked on it. Off the kitchen was a small pantry. We opened the window and pushed back the shutters. Along one wall was a row of wooden barrels, all empty except one that contained what looked like sand mixed with mouse droppings. It tasted like corn meal. On one shelf were items of kitchen ware, odd members of sets, wine glasses, all covered in dust and cobwebs. On another shelf were half-empty bottles of oil and vinegar, glass jars of icing sugar and powdered milk, oatmeal and chick peas, flour and baking powder, rice and dried apples. On the counter under the shelving were three bottles of preserves. We opened one, dug away the wax seal, and wolfed down what tasted like service berries. The sweetness of the fruit mingled with a vision of the place restored, saved from extinction, brought back to life."

"And now the vision is reality."

"Reality always falls short."

Janice called from the kitchen, "I could use some help in here."

Bernice frowned, turned her head, and shouted back, "In a minute."

He turned the page. The headline said *A Rap on Race*. He read aloud: "Some life and some light on deadly subjects like America, Race, The World, The Future, Where We Come From, What's Happening, by ... is it a black and a white, or a bright young man and a bright old lady? Foxy sweethearts." The "foxy sweethearts" (Margaret Mead and James Baldwin) were pictured opposite, looking impossibly young.

"Why bother with that old stuff? It might as well never have existed. I mean, *James Baldwin?* Come on."

Janice called again, "Bernice!"

Bernice licked the corner of her mouth. "Frailty, thy name is woman."

Christopher

*T*he dog, Sammy, was all eyes and ears on the porch, all bony hips and wagging, otter tail, until the stranger, Alden, passed by. Inside the door of the barn the two childen, laughing, chased Amy's pet rabbit, a black Netherland Dwarf rabbit, around in circles. It stood still, sniffing the air, until it felt the heat of a hand, or saw the rope of a braid hanging down, then it took a quick, high leap as if flicked by a strong middle finger and darted away. Amy, giggling, ran after it while Gabriele, going back, blocked its way. Blocked, it stood still, sniffing the air. The game ended when the animal tired and let itself be captured.

Inside the shed a yellow Mercedes Benz, vintage 1958 or 1959, sat on cement blocks, tireless, with the hood open and an oil-smudged cloth covering the front fender. The engine was dirt-caked and looked its age, in contrast to the rust-free body and clean interior. The shed smelled of engine oil. One match, and it could easily go up in flames. The window looked out onto the field and the woods.

Christopher came out of the woods and started across the field towards the house. The field was bright with many varieties of wildflowers. Every so often he stopped and picked a few. He was tall and thin and had that lumbering walk that reminded Alden of Peter Fonda in *Easy Rider.*

At supper the conversation felt forced and awkward. Clinton's name kept coming up, like the memory of a sore tooth. It was one day short of a week since his death. Bernice was worried about the effect on Gabriele. "Don't think too harshly of your father," she said. "He wasn't all bad."

Gabriele did not take her eye from the squirt of ketchup on her plate, into which she was about to dip a paper thin, crisp home fry.

"He did a lot of good work for us. For example, these cupboards." She made a sweeping motion with her hand while looking back over her shoulder to the left and right of the sink. "Even this table we're sitting at is his. An excellent carpenter."

"We never saw the other side of Clinton," Janice said. "He was always nice when he was here. We found out too late."

"When he beat us," Christopher said, working his jaw, "the son-of-a-bitch was always quotin' the Bible, as if that made it right. *Do not withhold discipline from a child; if you beat him with a rod, he will not die. If you beat him with a rod, you will save his life from Hell.*

"I know this much," Bernice said. "He was a hard worker, always willing to listen."

"The problem with Clinton was he didn't get along with his wife," Janice said. "He didn't understand her."

"Oh, he understood her well enough," Christopher said. "Trouble was, he didn't like what he understood."

"If he had understood her," Janice said, "he would have given her the life she wanted."

"He was a mean bastard. That's all I know and all I need to know, as someone once said. When he didn't get his way, he started swinging."

"Come on," Bernice said, "what do you say we cut this conversation. We didn't ask Alden out here to listen to a lot of bad shit about Clinton."

"Well, you talk then," Christopher said, glaring at her.

"All right, I'll talk." She glanced around. "Who wants some more chili?"

"I do!" the three children shouted, one after the other, like three successive notes on a xylophone.

Janice, nearest the big pot of chili, and its main author, did the honours. After the children, Alden also accepted a second helping. "The meat tastes different," he said.

"It's deer meat."

"I like it."

"Not too wild?"

He looked from Janice to Christopher and back to Janice. "Do you do much hunting, yourselves?"

"A little," Christopher answered.

"What do you hunt?"

"Deer, rabbit, pheasant, bear, skunk, you name it."

"Bear?"

"There's one thing you have to know when you go hunting. When you find your prey, you must not get between them and their habitual cover, because when they feel trapped, they will come right at you. They'll come so fast, you won't have time to think. Then the only thing that'll save you is luck."

"I thought deer, when they start, run away from you."

"I'm talkin' about bears, man. Bears."

"Oh."

"Let me tell you about the time me and my dad went huntin'. We was huntin' deer, but we didn't care that much what it was. Long as it was movin'. Well, I saw this here black squirrel sittin' up in a hemlock tree. So I shot it out of that tree and it fell, but it wasn't dead, and when I picked it up, the little sucker bit me clean through the ball of my thumb. Dirty little bugger, I said, and smacked his head against the tree. I showed my dad how he bit me, and he said, Suck it out clean and put some iodine on when you get home. Dirty little bugger, I said again, because it was startin' to hurt. Do you know what a bugger is, my dad asked me. We call anything a bugger, I said. A bugger is a man who has intercourse with animals, he said. It is an evil crime. I thought of various animals but none of them was that attractive or practical, that I could think of. If you so much as think about doin' it, you'll go to hell, he said. I was maybe twelve or thirteen at the time, so what did I know."

"Come on, kids, let's go upstairs," Bernice said with fire in her eyes. "There's something I want to show you." Teeth showing, she passed close behind Christopher's chair, as if looking for somewhere to kick it that would cause it to collapse.

Alden leaned across the table and spoke directly to Christopher. "Did you ever wonder why it is that dogs go around sniffing each other all the time? Well, I'll tell you how it happened. A long time ago, when dogs were fewer and wiser, instead of fighting, they would call a meeting. You know, to talk things over. Before going inside, though, each dog had to leave his asshole outside. Sort of like in Japan, you know, where the people take off their shoes. Same thing. Anyhow, this one time there was this big wind, really big, and it whirled all those assholes around and around and mixed them all up. Ever since that day, dogs have been going around trying to locate the asshole that used to belong to them."

Janice got up to clear the table. To keep herself from laughing out loud, she covered her mouth with the back of her hand. Christopher bared a crooked eye tooth, rubbed the side of a finger in the cleft of his chin, pushed his chair back, got up, and went outside. His heart in his throat, Alden backed into the living room.

Bernice put on a record. No one felt like talking. Janice brought the dessert from the kitchen, a chocolate mousse topped with whipped cream. The children came running back down the stairs, Amy first, with Gabriele close behind, not wanting to let her out of her sight, and Paul last. No one made a move to summon Christopher.

And no one saved him any dessert. They were angry with him, probably not for the first time. Alden helped in the kitchen with the dishes. When Bernice and Janice decided they wanted to be alone, they shooed him outside.

Christopher sat on the railing of the porch, sidesaddle. Alden sat on the top step. "You ain't bad with your mouth. How you with a shotgun?"

"Not bad."

"Is that so?"

"Yeah, it's so."

"Some of us plan to do some huntin' later. Care to join us?"

"Okay."

"You won't ever live to regret it."

"I'm wondering about Gabby though."

"No need to worry. She can sleep here, case we're late gettin' back."

"Right."

"Couple boys in town that's comin' along." He leaned over the railing and spat on the ground below. "I'll just run in and pick ' em up, then get back here for you all."

"I'll be here."

"Won't be but half an hour."

Christopher drove away in the truck, trailing a little cloud of dust. Alden stretched his legs. From the window of the kitchen he could hear the music Janice and Bernice were playing. Judy Collins was singing the song about her father from Ohio and the trip to Paris they almost never took. The black-faced dog came up, eyed him benevolently, and trotted off in the direction of the barn. He closed his eyes. His mind drifted off, in one direction, then in another, but always, while drifting, conscious of the many different sounds coming to him from outside himslf, as well as within.

Bear Hunt

*C*hristopher's two friends were named Gary and Wayne. Wayne was introduced as the star pitcher of the local softball team. Short, prematurely bald, his cheek bulging with a chew of tobacco, he didn't look like the star of anything, unless it was the crew of the local gas station. Only his big hands fit the description. Gary was thin, with large, round, nervous eyes and a little, scraggly goatee, like English ivy gone dry and crumbly.

He took one look and ordered Christopher to "get this city boy some shoes for his feet." Christopher sent Janice inside to look for a pair of boots, because back in the woods, where they were going, "there was more swamp than solid earth." Bernice came out with an old U.S. Army jacket and a knit cap for his head, so he would not catch his death of cold.

When he was outfitted, they sat on the back of the truck awhile, sipping beer and talking baseball. Then Christopher brought out the guns, and abruptly the mood turned serious. He handed Alden a single-shot Winchester .22.

"Every use a twenty-two?"

"Not in a good while."

"There ain't nothin' to it, so I guess you'll make out alright. Somebody'll be around to pick up the pieces."

They all piled into the pick-up and drove off into the darkness – Janice and Paul up front with Christopher, Alden in back with Gary and Wayne, Sammy at the tailgate, barking into the wind. At the T-intersection they turned right and went up another hill, past some farms, heading inland. Greenland was a collection of eight or ten houses, a couple of them no more than tar-papered shacks. After Greenland the asphalt gave way to dirt and the ride was exceedingly bumpy.

As the truck carried them over narrow dirt roads, past deserted farm houses, with rusted-out ploughs dropped as if in the middle of a day's work, the conversation picked up again, and the talk was about other trips, other kills, or near-kills. Soon the only light came from the moon, which was three-quarters full, and it was cool enough that Alden was grateful for the jacket and the cap. The truck swerved down and over a plank-wood bridge, then past a lake rimmed with boulders and scraggy thorn bushes.

"Better make time, cousin," Wayne said, rapping at the window. "Bear be done ate and gone home."

Christopher pulled over. Wayne and Gary grabbed their guns and jumped down. Christopher came around and began hauling equipment out from under a canvas: flashlights, shells, a bottle of rum. "Who gets what," he said.

"He can run with me," Gary said. "Let him carry the flashlight." Alden took the flashlight, the gun, and a swig from the bottle that was being passed around.

Janice, Paul, and Sammy were to accompany Christopher up the road and into the woods. Alden was to go with Wayne and Gary back down and around the lake, then uphill into the woods. Somewhere in the woods above the lake they would all meet.

Christopher, Gary, and Wayne had double-barreled shotguns, with .22 shells in one barrel and buckshot in the other. Janice and Paul had rifles like Alden. When everyone was loaded Christopher said, "Let's go. We'll meet up in about an hour. What time you got?"

Wayne checked his watch. "Nine o'clock."

"Good," Christopher said, setting off. "Don't shoot no cats."

"Shoot him if I see him," Gary said, leading the way down toward the lake.

Wayne followed Gary, and Alden trailed Wayne. They plunged through bushes, between clumps of dwarf spruce, into a scattering of burnt-out tamarack. Already the ground was wet, soggy wet. He focused on the back of Wayne's jacket until he realized that then he could not see anything else. If he was to grow used to the dark, he would have to look around at what there was to see.

It did not take him long to learn how to pick up his feet and miss the roots and an awkward stumble, or how to duck down and miss the branches that flew back from Wayne's hand into his face. Every few minutes Gary stopped and had him throw his flashlight across a tree trunk where it had fallen, on the path, or in a hollow, or on the hillside. He stood with his gun at the ready. If he saw anything, he didn't say so, and Alden was not about to ask. All he wanted to do was keep up and not get lost; be ready to shoot if they told him to shoot; stay alert in case they saw, or heard, a bear, or a cougar.

Overhead was the sound of an airplane, bending in from the Bay of Fundy toward Halifax. In the clear black sky he could see the red light flashing. It was the milk run from Saint John. In twenty minutes, or less, it would be down. The city, people, lights, laughter, were that close!

Gary stopped and knelt down. "Hush," he said, tilting his head into the wind. All he could hear was the faint rush of a brook in the woods and the rise and fall of a chorus of crickets. Gary whistled; a low whistle came in reply.

"Son of a bitch! Fox! Let's go!" He sprang away, and Wayne followed. Suddenly on the run, Alden felt panic. There was no way he could keep up with the others. His lungs ached. His boots felt like buckets of cement.

The moon went in and out of the milky clouds, making them glow, and he felt more and more tired. The distance between himself and Wayne widened all the time. He turned on his flashlight, trying to keep him in view. But on they pressed, through woods, through bogs, never breaking stride.

Miles, we must be covering miles.

The ground was soggy; he could feel water begin to soak through the old boots. At last he could see them no more. He could hear them no more. Then he made the mistake of stopping and sitting down instead of going on, at whatever pace. He sat against a tree for three or four minutes, out of breath. When he got up again he was so dizzy that he lost his balance after a step or two, and he fell. He sank down against the tree again and put his head back, surrendering to the fatigue.

Let them laugh if they want to. If I'm lost I can find my way out in the morning.

He lay the rifle across his legs, where he could reach it, and he held the flashlight in his right hand. Maybe there really were bears.

Clouds hurried by overhead, thicker now, blocking the light of the moon. He could barely see his own hands. The sound of rushing water seemed very near. As his body recovered from the long run he began to feel an intense glow of heat. Then this died, and the cold came on. His hands were like ice. Long, thin needles of ice jabbed his upper arms, his shoulders, and his chest. His teeth chattered, and he could not control the growing fear, though fear of what, he could not have said.

So his thoughts came now, more quickly, but jumbled, chopped. It had been a mistake to try to keep up with the others, when his whole body had told him to stay back. He had been too worried about the dark. What was the dark? It was only a temporary thing. It was already ten, already eleven. The main thing was to keep warm, stay alert, not panic. Where was he, after all? Five miles from the coast? Six? He could walk that far. Kejumkujik was the other way, a bit farther perhaps, but not too far. He'd find campers, canoeists, families, campfires, food, help.

Right here, where I'm sitting, it isn't so bad. The lake is clear, unpolluted. I could almost live here, if I had some shelter, a little cabin, a geodesic dome. Jason would love it ... Annalisa ...

He was sleeping now. And in his sleep he dreamed. He dreamed he was on his way to visit a friend, and the friend lived in a very tall apartment building, in a city of very tall apartment buildings and businesses. But he could not remember which floor he lived on. They all seemed identical. Long, wide, busy corridors, where children played, skipping rope, riding tractors, leaping from foot to foot in a game of hopscotch. At an open door he stopped and looked inside. A man and a woman were arguing. When he realized he was intruding on something that was none of his business, something very private, he moved away, but it was too late. The man had seen him. He began running. The man followed, waving a gun, shouting for him to stop. He ducked into a stairwell and ran up the stairs to the next floor. The door was locked. He ran up the stairs to the next floor. The door was locked. He was so tired. He sat on the step, with his head down. All he could do was wait now, for the man with the gun.

But instead of the man with the gun, the person who came up the stairs was his son, Jason. His eyes were much bigger than before, and black all around, as if painted. Then it was not hard cement he was sitting on, but soft wood, and he was home, on Walnut Street, sitting in the chair at the bottom of the stairway, the day he had his heart attack, and he was asking Jason through the balustrade to do something please, he was dying. Jason had thick lips, like a eight-year-old thunderstruck boy about to bestow a kiss; but before he could speak, Alden brought his two hands up and just had time to catch the wire that was being fastened around his neck.

It cut like a razor into his fingers. It cut so deeply into the skin that he had to let go. The wire tightened again and took his breath. He heard a voice say, "Too bad you didn't just butt out," and he knew he had drawn the last sweet air the world had left for him. A burst of lights danced before his eyes. Images came and went. He saw Jason and Lisa waiting at the station for the train to come in, with his body, and it filled him with such sadness to be dying in this way, at the hands of a stranger, without even knowing why, that he relaxed and in that instant he felt his neck muscles relax too and there was a fraction of a second during which the wire was loose enough for him to gasp but it was a living breath this time, and something in his brain came alive, and he grabbed the Winchester by his side, cocked it, turned it up, and pulled the trigger.

The blast split the night in two. Gary, whimpering like a young, inexperienced boy in sexual excitement, staggered back into the moonlight. The blood spouted, like water from a pipe, from his face, what was left of his face for the shot had taken his lower jaw straight off. He held his arms out from his side and moved them up and down like pump handles, as if to pump the blood with more force.

He slumped to the ground, with a sad, faraway look, and was still. Alden was on his feet again. Gun in hand, he started back, toward the lake. Thirty feet on, he stopped dead in his tracks, remembering that he had yet to re-load the gun. He fumbled in his pocket for a shell.

He no longer felt any fear. He could go on now, as long as need be, as far as need be. He was on the go but no longer on the run. He was wide awake. He existed beyond any ideas he might ever have had of right and wrong, good and bad, just and unjust. He himself, in reality, did not even exist. His body existed, the world existed, he had hopes and fears. He had friends and enemies. He himself, as a solid, stable entity, did not exist. He had never existed, as such. He would never exist, as such. Existence, conceived thus and so, could never hold him.

The wind gusted. The moon shook in the trees. Above the trees a half-sky of stars glowed vaguely, distantly in the unsettled air. The moon tasted of salt and the smell in the funeral seaweed was of childbirth and charnel house. What did his nothingness seek? A changing of his shirt and his skin and his hair and his calling: it was good to sink in the earth a little, the mud. It was fitting to put out of mind the betrayers, the friends asleep on their comfortable couches, while he sojourned among trees and leafage, and his skin felt like metal, like armour, resistant to cold, to knives, to razor blades, to everything that cuts.

On the surface of the lake stones floated like dead fish in the moonlight. The road was on the other side of the lake. He could hear voices. Christopher and Janice stood by the back of the truck, talking. A half dozen rabbits hung upside down from the outside mirror on the driver's side. Sammy followed Paul up the road, while Paul called the names of the missing men. He barked at the sound of the names, as if that would bring them back.

Alden stood at the edge of the woods, looking up the road towards the boy and the dog, but listening to the talk at the back of the truck. "I mean, she just assumes she's running the show," Janice said.

"Here's one show she's not running. Never did, never will."

"I've had it. I say, let's dump the bitch."

"Yes, let's do."

"When I think of all the shit I've had to take ..."

"Nobody'll know the difference."

"There's Paul."

"Fuck Paul."

"Yeah, fuck Paul. Fuck them all."

"So we get the stuff and split. Okay?"

"What did the man say?"

"The boat gets in tomorrow night. Same place as last time."

"How much has he got?"

"Two tons."

"That'll do."

"Sssh." Paul came back down the hill towards the truck.

"Any sign of them?"

"No."

Christopher looked up at the midnight sky. "Beats the hell outta me," he said, kicking the gravel.

They waited another twenty minutes and when Gary and Wayne did not come, they got into the truck and drove away.

Alden came out onto the road and watched the lights of the truck as they disappeared into the darkness. He started walking. He walked and walked. At the top of a hill he stopped and listened. When he heard nothing, he threw the gun away, into the bushes. Then he walked on.

Everything He Wanted Him to Hear

*T*he line-up of cars approaching the exit ramp of the underground parking complex was long, snaking from the basement level to ground level, and to the level above that. Alden was far enough back, around a pillar, that he could not see the booth where the attendant waited to take payment. At the window of his car a voice said imperatively, "Cigarette, if you please." It was as if whoever it was thought he could take a stranger by surprise and make him fork out.

"No," he said, anxiously. "I have nothing at all." He could feel enmity fuming up all around him like smoke.

"Got something to eat," another voice said, and when he didn't answer, "Got something to eat!" Suddenly, from behind, came the sound of an explosion – a gun being fired. He knew that a gunman was on the loose, even in this crowded darkness, systematically shooting everyone on the way out. *He's killing everyone, without exception. Nowhere to hide. No escape.* Just as the gunman leaned in to have a look into the window of his car, he awoke.

*L*ord Randall looked like a mass of old wool that had been matted together in the mud down by the river. One eye was half-closed, because a muscle had been ripped in a fight. He had blood on his foreleg. He smelled like a fish. "You're filthy," Hattie said to him, pouring the milk out to cool in his dish. "Filthy old thing. Where have you been?" He often stayed out all night and she thought nothing of it. The kitchen window was left open, for his return, which normally took place before dawn. But this morning, when she got up, he had not come back. It was after eight when he finally hauled himself up to the box below the window, too tired even to make the leap from box to window.

It was strangely quiet, this Wednesday morning. Lord Randall, having stayed out all night, was too tired to make his usual fuss. "That'll teach you, wicked old cat. Staying out all night; leaving Hattie alone all night." He drank his milk without looking at her, as if ashamed; or worried she might lash out. He drank it all and went away somewhere to lick his wounds and clean up.

Meredith was gone for good. She had departed before breakfast, expressing a desire to "live cheek by jowl with her subject." (Hattie understood this to mean that she had concluded, upon available evidence, that Elk River was not the "Switzerland of Nova Scotia" the guide book had wanted her to believe it was.) Alan had finished his breakfast but not until satisfying his desire to share a little of everything with "this poor beat-up country cat, whose only sin is to be alive." With Lord Randall's disappearing act, Alan also disappeared up the stairs to pack and get ready to go. (He would be leaving for Yarmouth, to catch the ferry to Bar Harbour, Maine, from where he would proceed inland, to the cabin he'd rented, and his hoped-for rendezvous with his fisherman-son.)

Alden was still in bed, not sleeping but unable to move. He had come in a little after five and climbed the stairs to his room. Every step he took the stairs creaked. He had just enough strength to pull off his filthy jeans and his shirt before collapsing on the bed. At eight thirty he tried to get up, but he ached everywhere. He remembered the events of last night and thought he had dreamed them. But the mud-splattered jeans and the blood-soaked shirt on the floor were real, and so the events of the night before had to be real. He sank back on the bed.

Hattie started up the stairs, in her slow, careful way, testing each sore, arthritic foot as she went. Before she reached the fourth step the phone rang.

Bernice wanted to talk to Alden. "They went hunting after supper, Alden, Janice, Christopher, and a couple of the boys. We haven't seen him since."

"He's upstairs. He's not feeling well."

"He must have got lost in the woods, it was pretty dark."

"Do you want to talk with him?"

"Don't bother. The thing is, we've got Gabriele with us, and she's nervous about being left alone."

"Bring the child here to me," Hattie said, quick to see what had to be done. "In the meantime I'll give the sister a call."

"Bless you."

Hattie cleared the dining room table. She re-set Alden's plate in the kitchen. She put on a fresh pot of coffee, to be ready when he came down. While she waited she listened to the radio and washed dishes. In the milky suds her hands looked old, the skin loose, like a false skin that could be peeled off. She held one of her hands up in front of her and turned it around for inspection. The knuckles were gray and swollen, with bumpy ridges like grape seeds under wraps.

"Maybe I *will* get that dishwasher I've been promising myself," she said, aloud.

*J*anice drove Alden's Volvo, with Gabriele next to her in the front seat. Bernice followed in the pick-up. Gabriele got out of the car and went straight to the front door of the house without waiting for Janice. Hattie gathered the child to her side. Bernice came to the bottom of the steps and looked up at Gabriele with an expression almost beatific. "You're here now," she said, and made a gesture with her two arms as if to embrace the whole house. Her eyes for one second raced up to the top of the wedding-cake facade. "You're safe."

Janice honked, and Bernice turned again, walked quickly to the truck, got in, and drove away.

Alden watched from the window. When they were gone, he put on a fresh shirt and the pair of new-bought jeans he' d worn at the funeral. He stuffed his old jeans and shirt into a plastic bag and rolled the bag into the backpack he' d brought along. He came down the stairs. Hattie sat with Gabriele at the table in the kitchen, by the open window. Gabriele was eating a bowl of cereal. Hattie sipped a cup of tea. Music played on the radio.

"How did you sleep," Hattie said.

"Fine." He was hardly able to talk but this did not seem to matter.

"There's bacon and pancakes."

"No. Just coffee."

Gabriele sat forward, with her head over her bowl, eating spoonfuls of rice crispies. She sipped milk from the bowl, milk that was the colour of mud because Hattie used brown sugar instead of white. With a little tilt of her head she looked at him, in a way that said, "Yes, I know you care about me, but I'm not at all sure I can trust you."

"Maybe I should call your sister and tell her where you are."

"Hattie did," was all she said.

Hattie came around and poured him a cup of coffee. "Here, this will warm you up."

He drank half a cup, warming himself inside and out. "There's someone I have to see ..."

"You go ahead. Gabby can stay here with me until Susan comes." She looked at Gabriele. "We'll be just fine, won't we?"

"Yes," Gabriele said, in a voice that was more like a whimper.

*F*rom a pay phone outside the greasy spoon by the bridge he called a lawyer he knew in Halifax. An hour later he met two provincial policemen in an unmarked car in the parking lot behind the Baptist church hallway up the hill above the river. He told them what had happened during the night, in so far as he understood it. He told them of his own theory, as to why someone would have wanted to kill him.

They searched the woods for two hours until they found Gary's body. It was not where Alden had thought it would be. It was farther up the hill, away from the lake. Three, four, then half a dozen additional police came through the woods to where the body was found. Later, the sheriff and his deputy, Roy, came along the soggy path through the snapping branches of the spruce, the birch, and the hemlock.

Responsible not just for Annapolis Royal, but for the surrounding area, including Elk River, the sheriff was not happy he hadn't been called earlier. "One fucking phone call," he said. "That's all it takes, one fucking phone call." The other police stopped what they were doing and looked at him. Roy stepped away, as if embarrassed at his outburst.

"Go ahead, tell him," one of the policemen said. "Tell him what you told us."

"I'll tell him what I know for sure." Alden told the sheriff everything he wanted him to hear about what had happened.

When he was done, the sheriff shook his head. "It's hard to figure. Why would anyone want to harm *you*, of all people?"

"That's what I'm trying to understand."

"Roy, you better get in here and take some of this down."

Roy, with his thin, delicate fingers, which seemed to shine with some sort of nail polish, pulled a pad of paper from his pant's pocket. "Okay, shoot," he said, when he was ready. The sheriff did the asking.

"Now, just what time did this attempt on your life take place?"

"Ten. Eleven. Around that time."

"You say, somebody tried to strangle you?"

"With a wire."

"And somehow you managed to fight him off?"

"Yes."

"Anything else?"

"One more thing. When I came to the edge of the woods I heard Christopher and Janice at the back of the truck. They didn't know I was there. They were talking about a shipment of drugs that's coming in tonight."

"Now, there's something to go on. Roy, have you got all that?"

"Almost."

"Did they say where it's supposed to come in? This shipment of drugs you mentioned?"

"All I heard them say was same place as last time."

"When they go to meet that boat, we'll be right fuck up their asses. If these here folks from the province care to tag along, won't nobody here raise much of a stink."

The sheriff and Roy led the way out of the woods, followed by Alden and the two policemen he' d come with. Several police remained at the site.

Watchers

Alden climbed the hill above the police station and wandered along Main Street toward the edge of town. He admired the big old comfortable houses, with their extensive front lawns and tall shade trees, set against the background of the wide, gently sloping valley.

Some of these houses were still occupied by descendents of the Loyalists who had fled here, to Annapolis Royal, during and after the American Revolution. He tried to imagine what these early refugees must have felt, seeing the wide, peaceful valley for the first time. On the evidence of these well-make structures, he concluded that they had not come as a defeated or disheartened people, but armed with some vision of their own, in some measure comparable to that of the people they were fleeing.

At the edge of town he stopped and gazed at the low, green mountains in the distance. When it was time, he turned and walked back to the station.

The black Valiant sat idling by the side of the road, a hundred yards south of the T-intersection, with a clear view across the scraggy corn field to The Farm. Half a mile behind the Valiant, two unmarked police cars sat idling under a shade tree. A little after seven Bernice and Christopher came out of the house, got into the pick-up, and drove off, turning north onto the road, in the direction of Elk River. The black Valiant pulled out and followed at a distance. The two unmarked police cars stayed back.

Through town and out the other side the pick-up followed the highway along the river towards Digby. At Digby it turned left onto the 101 and went as far as Weymouth North. It cut through Weymouth North until it came to a street leading down to a dock, close to where a river, the Sissiboo, emptied into the bay.

Christopher walked out onto the dock. A seiner was tied to a post at the far end. He climbed down into the boat and when he had searched it and found it empty, he whistled for Bernice to come down. Bernice got out of the truck, crossed the length of the dock, and climbed into the boat. Christopher started the motor. He backed the boat away from the dock, turned it around, and headed out into the bay.

One police car drove onto the dock and parked there. The second police car followed the Valiant along the coastal road, in the same direction as the boat that was headed into open water. But after a few miles, where the road curved inland, away from the shore, the sheriff almost lost sight of his quarry. He turned and found a rough driveway onto a spit of land overlooking the bay. He drove as far as he could, nestling the car in among the alder bushes and the shrub maple and the shrub oak. The two of them, the sheriff and Roy, walked the rest of the way to the edge of the cliff.

From this high ground, with binoculars, they could see across the bay to Digby Neck. The evening sky, beyond the peninsula, turned red as the sun set. Below, anchored in the middle of the bay, the fishing boat held fast. They flattened themselves on the ground to wait. They waited an hour, then two, and nothing happened. The hard-packed earth hurt them in the gut and in the ribs.

Farther back, away from the cliff, on the hillside above the alder bushes and the shrub maple and the shrub oak, the grass was delicately pale, almost lemon-coloured. The perfect patterns of grass against sea calmed, yet excited him in a way he had never experienced before. An unassailable optimism flowed in him like adrenalin. Perhaps it was adrenalin – no more than that. Time passed, but he did not lose the edge that he had. It was part of him now.

Alden watched the watchers. The sky, as it shaded into purple, looked very close, like a theatrical backdrop. A yacht appeared stage left, in the mouth of the bay. Puffs of black smoke rose from the stack of the fishing boat, as Christopher prepared to receive the incoming vessel.

The two boats tied on, and various crew on the yacht began unloading to the seiner. The sheriff, with a few words to his deputy, signaled it was time to call in the Coast Guard. Roy walked a few paces towards the car, pulling his hat down on his forehead like a baseball player coming up to bat. As if in slow motion he pulled his gun out of his belt, and turned to face the sheriff, his chin shoved forward, the nose long and straight like a wedge. The sheriff, keeping watch over the bay, felt something at his back. "What's the matter, Roy?"

Roy raised the gun higher, aiming it at the sheriff. "Sucker."

"What's this?"

"This, my friend, is the end of the line."

"Fuck all, I never figured you."

"You never figured lots of things."

"No wonder we never found nothin' when we raided them time and time again."

"Like I say, lots of things you never figured."

"It was you that killed Clinton."

"Now why would I want to do somethin' dumb like that."

"Because he found out what was going on."

"Wrong again."

"Christopher?"

"So what?"

"Why?"

"Found out the old man was beatin' up on the kid. Went crazy."

"How much do you get out of it?"

"We'll talk about that some other time. Move on back there a little closer to that cliff. If you don't fall, I might have to shoot you."

But the shot that rang out came from behind a boulder thirty yards away, between the cliff and the various bushes and shrubs. Roy gave a cry and the gun fell to the ground.

The sheriff, coming close, looked at him with disgust. "You were my righthand man."

"I was never your man, right hand or left hand. I was your dog. Whatever you said I was supposed to lap it up."

A coast guard boat, cutting across the water from the tip of the peninsula, moved in behind the yacht. It took several minutes for the people on the yacht to realize they were being tracked. At the last moment they cut themselves free from the fishing boat and made a run for it along the shore, where they were met by a second coast guard boat, which allowed no escape.

Mistake!

Christopher's lips did not seem to move with his words, and the harder she stared at them, the more unsure she was of their shape, or what the shape might mean. The deck was slippery with a heavy, unpleasant scent she had trouble placing. She laboured to remember something she may only have dreamed: twisted roots, petals like rubber, phosphorescent fish.

The tremor of fear passed. Except for his complete beardlessness there was nothing frightening about the man. She had broken the backs of bulls stronger by far than he was. She felt the door with her fingertips and it burst, jumped away like a frightened rabbit, and she plunged into the silent, candle-lit cabin, swollen with excitement, bloodlust, and a foreboding that mingled in her brain like the conviction that the end was near, his most likely, hers possibly.

In her hand she held the orange crowbar, and the man fell back, afraid. Burning, half-crazy with hate, she moved towards him, and she was like a snake, coiled to strike. She struck! A shock went through her. Mistake! It was a trick! His eyes were open, cold-bloodedly watching her to see how she worked. His eyes pinned her as his hand pinned her arm. Never before, she thought, have I experienced a grip like this. Her whole arm burned. It was as if his enveloping fingers were viper's fangs, shooting poison. They struggled, opposite each other, grotesquely shaking hands, dear, long-lost brother and sister. She felt bones go, torn from their sockets; she screamed. For a split second he relaxed his grip, and she shook free.

229

She ran up the steps onto the deck.

In his eyes a fire leaped. He flew at her. Suddenly, darkness. She was falling through space, snatching at the huge twisted roots of an oak, down, down.

And something still worse. He was whispering, spilling words like buckets of molten iron ore, his mouth two inches from her ear. She refused to listen. His syllables licked at her. His whispering followed her into the water, though she had out-fought him. "It was an accident," she barked back. "Blind, mindless, mechanical."

She was huge with half the sea in her mouth. No one would follow her now. She tumbled down, clutching with her one weak arm at the roots of the twisted oak. She seemed to recognize the place, but it was impossible. "It was an accident," she whispered. She seemed to desire to fall, and though she did not stop fighting it, she knew she could never win. She looked down, down, into a darkness that was bottomless, as from the edge of a cliff. Incredibly, she felt herself moving towards it, wanting it.

Christopher was alone in the boat. He steered it away from the yacht, towards shore. A policeman slid down the face of the cliff to the narrow, pebble beach, but got there too late. Christopher was already out of the boat and running towards the far end of the beach. The policeman called for him to stop. He fired a shot, but missed.

Alden ran along the top of the cliff, and though he could not always see Christopher on the beach below, he could hear him, scattering pebbles in his flight. He was sure-footed in the shallow-rooted grass. He was young again, with a spring to his step he had not experienced in years. There was no limit to how far he could go, or how fast. He was in the game now, and the rules of the game were made for him to follow and transcend.

The beach narrowed, and came to an end. There was nowhere to go. Christopher scrambled to the top of the cliff. Surprise! Alden was not dead, not even half-dead. His eyes were open: he was alive, alert, and on top of him! It was not the root of a tree that Christopher had hold of, but the foot of a man. They struggled.

Locked together, they rolled down the slope of the cliff, through sandy grass, over scrub maple, across loose pebble, onto sea-slimed rock. As one, they slipped down, into the smooth, green-bottoming water. Alden let go.

Fifty feet off shore a boat floated, white, with blue trim. Behind them, on the beach, another shot rang out, a warning. *Can I swim that far?* He looked at Alden but found no answer. *If I breath out, will it be my last breath?*

With his foot he pushed against something slippery-alive. Rising up out of the water, he took one last gulp of air, and dived.

Imagine

She was as enthusiastic as ever, but something in the way she sat there made her look frail. Her head was bent to one side as she wrote. Her back was rounded, hunched forward, so that the tip of one shoulder almost touched the ear on the side of the head that was twisted down. Her cheek was fresh, pink, as if recently rubbed; but below the eyes, across the cheekbones, crow's feet branched, and there was on her, at moments like these, the same dark look, of disillusion. The mouth was shut hard, the chin set forward, the eyes small and grey and unfocused, like the pods of snails.

With his bill in hand, Hattie came out into the hallway, but he was no longer there. She removed her glasses, dropped them to dangle from the black elastic band around her neck. Lord Randall, crouching in the doorway of the kitchen, gazed at her. "Where did he go?" she said, but instead of answering, Lord Randall stuck his tongue out, and began a vigorous licking of the upper reaches of his left foreleg. "You're not a bit of help, as usual," Hattie said, and went outside.

The trunk of his car was open. Below the house, at the roadside, he waited, looking across the town, across the river, at the church, or the part of the church that was visible above the treeline. "Look," he said, when he saw her coming down. "See how high she rises above the town. Imagine, there are streets below her, and houses, and people, all hidden."

"So there are!" Hattie exclaimed, bright with life again. But he had seen her sitting there, hunched at her desk, her face and eyes fixed, vacant, with disillusion. And the crow's feet near her eyes, and her mouth shut so hard that he had had to come away.

They settled the bill as they walked back up to the car. He closed the trunk and got in. "I think she's *lucky*," Hattie said, at the window, "to be going back with you."

"I'm sure *we're* the lucky ones."

"The child needs a home, after all she's been through. A stable home."

"I don't know if stability is what we have to offer. But whatever it is, it's a lot."

He started the motor. Hattie stepped back. "I wish you well."

On the road, at the bottom of the driveway, he stopped and looked back up at the house, to see Hattie already climbing the steps. He poked his head out the window and called, "Good-bye!"

In the ornate entrance, below the double dormer, below the double bell-cast roof, Hattie waved one last time, with her small hand. Her face, that moved between brightness and sadness, was gone.

Pointless

*H*oward made the dog sit before he would let him see the green tennis ball again. The sun was high above the barn, and already Sammy was hot and tired, from chasing Howard's ball so many times into the field on the other side of the barn. But Howard wasn't ready to quit. He was having too much fun. Sammy was a fine dog, friendly, anxious to please, and Howard felt like a boy again, romping with his first pet. Sometimes, in a teasing mood, he would only pretend to throw the ball, and Sammy would spend minutes searching where the ball should have landed, before coming back crestfallen. It was more fun when Stevie threw the ball, because then he could run back and forth, maybe even down the hill by the side of the barn with the ball in his mouth, and Stevie would chase after him, and follow him everywhere, even into the woods, and if he shouted at him, it was always because he was having a good time, not because he was mad, or teasing.

Edna, at the back door of the house, had to do some shouting of her own, before Howard was able or willing to hear her, though he was no more than a hop, skip, and a jump away. "... talk to you!"

Howard wheeled around. "What!" He cupped a hand behind an ear.

"Someone on the phone wants to talk to you!"

"Who!"

"That man that's come to take Gabriele away!"

"What does he want!"

"He wants to say good-bye!"

While they talked, Sammy, ears cocked, kept looking at the ball and reproachfully at Howard. *What a time to choose to talk! I'm too hot to do nothing but sit here and stare. I need some action. Either he throws the ball, or I find some shade.*

Howard handed the ball to Stevie. "You throw him a few."

Howard went inside, and Stevie was in command. He tossed the ball up in the air a few times, to prove Sammy's patience. "So, you want the ball, do you?" Sammy barked loudly, demanding an end to all pointless questions.

Stevie came around the front of the barn and stood at the top of the driveway. Sammy came and sat by his side without being told. Stevie held the ball above his head, shoulder back, elbow twisted in a funny way. "Are you ready?" With the same motion as a javelin thrower might use, he sent the ball flying toward the dirt road at the end of the driveway.

When he looked down, Sammy was already gone, halfway to the road, in hot pursuit. He had decided not to wait for the boy to release him (as he knew he was supposed to), because he had already waited long enough, and besides, the boy, in his new-found sense of himself as "master" if not of the dog then of the situation, had forgot his part of the bargain.

Poor Soldier

Read us a story, the children begged Susan, the moment the door was shut and all the parents had gone home. So Susan read them a story called "Twelve Daughters."

There was once upon a time a King who had twelve daughters, each more beautiful than the other. They all slept together in one room, in which their beds stood side by side, and every night when they were in them the King locked the door, and bolted it. But in the morning when he unlocked the door, he saw that their shoes were worn out with dancing, and no one could find out how that had come to pass.

The children all sat around Susan on the couch, four girls and two boys, ranging in age from four years to eight years. Even the oldest boy, David, showed interest, sitting on the arm of the couch, looking across the book on Susan's lap to the girl cuddled next to her, for this was Gabriele's last day with them, and on the last day, no matter who it was, he knew he should think of the other person, not himself.

Then the King caused it to be proclaimed that whosoever could discover where they danced at night, should choose one of them for his wife and be King after his death, but that whosoever came forward and had not discovered it within three days and nights, should have forfeited his life. It was not long before a King's son presented himself, and offered to undertake the enterprise. He was well received, and in the evening was led into a room adjoining the princesses' sleeping-room. His bed was placed there, and he was to observe where they went and danced, and in order that they might do nothing secretly or go away to some other place, the door of their room was left open.

"He got hisself an eyeful I bet," David said, and Susan smiled.

"If they had any secrets I guess they didn't have any when he was done with them."

"Ssssh," the other children said.

But the eyelids of the prince grew heavy as lead, and he fell asleep, and when he awoke in the morning, all twelve princesses had been to the dance, for their shoes were standing there with holes in the soles. On the second and third nights there was no difference, and his head was struck off without mercy.

"Why did he always fall asleep?"

"Wait – you'll see."

Many others came after this and undertook the enterprise, but all forfeited their lives. Now it came to pass that a poor soldier, who had a wound, and could serve no longer, found himself on the road to the town where the King lived.

Susan's voice was getting hoarse: she fingered the remaining pages rapidly. She was rushing a little now, to finish, since it was already ten o'clock, when Alden had said he would come by.

There he met an old woman, who asked him where he was going. "I hardly know myself," answered he, and added in jest: "I had half in mind to discover where the princesses danced their shoes into holes, and thus become King." "That is not so difficult," said the old woman. "You must not drink the wine which will be brought to you at night, and must pretend to be sound asleep." With that she gave him a cloak, and said, "If you wear this, you will be invisible, and then you can steal after the twelve." When the soldier had received this good advice, he fell to in earnest, took heart, went to the King, and announced himself as a suitor.

"If he's invisible, he'll be able to see – everything!"

"Maybe not such a good idea, eh?"

He was conducted that evening at bed-time into his room, and as he was about to go to bed, the eldest came and brought him a cup of wine, but he had tied a sponge under his chin, and let the wine run down into it, without drinking a drop.

On the street in front of the house a car honked. "David, look and see if that's the man come to fetch Gabriele."

The boy got up from the arm of the couch, went over, and looked out the window. Out of a two-door, red Volvo climbed a bearded man, in blue jeans and a white dress shirt with rolled-up sleeves.

"It's him," he said, and squatted beside the window, while behind him came the muffled sound of small girls filing from the room, into the hallway, to greet the stranger.

Fortune Cookie

The red Volvo was parked diagonally against the curb, across from the turn-off to the Canadian Forces Base at Greenwood. In the window of the Chinese Restaurant its reflection was superimposed on the people and the fixtures inside.

At the table by the window, behind white, transparent curtains, a man and a child sat together, eating lunch. They had been inside for the best part of an hour, and the car was suffering. Parked in direct sunlight, with all the windows rolled up, it was getting very hot inside. Honk! It went, not once but twice. Still, they didn't come.

The man asked for a cup of green tea. The car moaned.

Finally, the bill came. On the plastic tray were two fortune cookies. The girl decided to save hers for the car. The man opened his and read his fortune, in smudged-blue mimeograph print: *Be on Look-Out for Very Big Change in Life.*

He folded the message twice, until it was no bigger than a nickel, and he put it into the pocket of his shirt. They stood up.

Acknowledgements

An earlier version of this novel won first prize in the 1986 Writers' Federation of Nova Scotia competition.

About the Author

Edward Lemond grew up in Indiana and California and came to Canada in 1969. After 24 years in Halifax he moved to Moncton, New Brunswick. He owned and operated the Attic Owl Bookshop for twenty-one years, in Halifax and in Moncton. From 2000 through 2011 he was a principal organizer for the annual Frye Festival in Moncton. He has published poems and short stories in various Canadian literary journals. He has written four novels, one novella, three poetry collections, and one book of short stories.

www.ingramcontent.com/pod-product-compliance
Lightning Source LLC
Chambersburg PA
CBHW050420260626
47156CB00003B/1094